C000259553

Richard Foreman is the autho[r] ... books, including *Augustus: Son* ... historical crime novellas. He is also the author of *Warsaw*, ... novel set during the end of the Second World War. He lives in London.

PRAISE FOR RICHARD FOREMAN:

'*Augustus: Son of Rome* forges action and adventure with politics and philosophy. This superb story is drenched in both blood and wisdom - and puts Foreman on the map as the coming man of historical fiction' - Saul David, Author of the *Zulu Hart* series

'Classy, humorous and surprisingly touching tales of cricket, friendship and crime.' - David Blackburn, *The Spectator*

'A rattling good yarn, requiring only the minimum of suspension of belief, and leaves one eagerly anticipating the next instalment of the adventures of the team as they accompany the King to Harfleur' - Major Gordon Corrigan, author of *A Great and Glorious Adventure: A Military History of the Hundred Years War*

A HERO
OF OUR TIME

RICHARD FOREMAN

For Hannah,
Best wishes.

R F

ENDEAVOURINK

AN ENDEAVOUR INK PAPERBACK

First published by Endeavour Press
in 2012

This paperback edition published in 2017
by Endeavour Ink
Endeavour Ink is an imprint of Endeavour Press Ltd
Endeavour Press, 85-87 Borough High Steet,
London, SE1 1NH

ISBN 978-1-911445-26-5

Printed and bound in Great Britain by
Clays Ltd, St Ives plc

www.endeavourpress.com

CHAPTER ONE

Captain Robert Fischer sat with his back to the window of course, so that the afternoon sun shone with spite into the eyes of all his appointments. The jaundiced beams, like metal scraping upon glass, screeched into the listless aspect presently of one Jakob Levin. A bovine, ursine-faced Wehrmacht Private was also present in the musty room. The guard was ornamental, yet also deemed essential.

"You are Jakob Levin, or rather 1556321?" the officer issued, following his statement up with a weary sigh which seemed part affected, part sincere.

"Yes, Herr Captain."

"You were a teacher I see?" the handsome officer then lazily inquired, as if already bored by the interview. He closed his eyes, as if suffering from a headache – or wishing that the whole world might disappear.

"I am a teacher, yes Herr Captain," Jakob replied, nodding his head and squinting in the light of the mustard sun.

"You were a teacher. Now you are, unfortunately, mine," Fischer exclaimed, raising his eyebrows and pursing his pink lips as he did so. If the directive, worded as a request, had come down from anyone less senior in rank then Robert might have fought or bribed his way out of the burden of nurse-maiding the prisoner. It was an inconvenience to say the least for the bachelor, who valued both his privacy and life of leisure. But the Wehrmacht officer had acceded to the order.

"Yes Herr Captain, I was a Professor of English," Jakob calmly stated whilst vigorously fighting off the compulsion to scratch his lice-infested scalp.

Although an English tutor and translator of David Hume, Jakob Levin had learned to relegate the importance of quibbling over semantics, especially if winning the argument meant receiving a rifle-butt in between the shoulder blades by an ignorant Nazi (if ignorance is malevolence, as well as bliss). Jakob often remembered, with mixed feelings as to the value of their teachings, how the rabbis and elders would drill into their flock in the camp that, 'All that matters is survival, neither dwell on the past or dream about the future. Concentrate on surviving the morning, then the afternoon, then the night.' Rebellion or resignation brought one the same fate, Jakob concluded.

"But as misfortunate as you are Jakob, some might judge you lucky. As inferior as you are our glorious state still considers you to be an essential worker," the Captain remarked, his tone laced with a harlequined irony – as well as a more obtuse mocking spirit. When the officer pronounced these last two words, he couldn't help but survey the reaction upon the old man's face. Robert Fischer was surprised at its lack of response. It had made the

German half-smile in the past when *they* had responded to him as if he were an angel when he had delivered those words, particularly of late. But this Jakob Levin had reacted with indifference, perhaps too much indifference. Robert did not doubt the stories of veterans on the Front suffering from a warped form of shell shock, oblivious to the tumult of bullets scorching and zipping around their ears. Could this sallow-faced Jew here be similarly desensitised to despair and hope? Certainly, in theory, the once philosophical German held his life as but a word.

"Should you have had a conversation with any friends or family, or your wife, just previous to your transfer here then it was, unfortunately, your last."

Still the former lauded academic remained stone-faced. But he was Jewish, 'too furtive to be dumb' the propaganda asserted. The prisoner was receptive, if inexpressive.

"There is but one more grief-filled existence to that of being a widow Jakob – that of being a widow who still believes she could be a wife," the officer intoned, privately impressed with the swiftness and originality of the cruel remark.

Jakob retained his squinting, almost gormless composure, to the Captain's slight interest and annoyance. The fish did not appear to be biting. But it was only a matter of time, or method, before Robert would pull out the right lure from his box. It was a game to the captain to uncover and then squeeze someone's weak spot. Even Achilles had his heel, Robert posed to himself, whilst at the same time believing in his own invulnerability.

"If you haven't already been told, you are to remain now in this house, albeit in my basement. There you will work, eat and sleep. I have been instructed from on high to employ you as a translator. I am to be sent various works of English Literature, mainly poetry I gather, and you are to translate them in to German."

Robert wondered if this brittle, gummy remnant of a man, still dressed in his threadbare camp uniform, also knew of the project by the Ministry Of Propaganda, entitled 'Death of the Author', to Germanise Europe's finest works of literature and art? Robert was intrigued because he too had shown a similar outward resignation to the crime that the Jew here exemplified. When asked some weeks ago as to how Robert knew he had gold in his soul, the officer had drily replied, "Because gold my dear, does not react to anything."

Rhythmically and nonchalantly, as if reciting a shopping list, the captain further informed the prisoner of his brief.

"If you refuse to do what has been requested of you, you will be shot. If your work proves unsatisfactory you will be shot. And (and here Robert looked straight into, almost behind, his appointment's aspect) if you bore me you will be shot."

Jakob raised a black, wiry eyebrow. The absurdism, horror and aphasia of the grotesque times outside were compounded by a statement at which the ageing Jew did not know whether to smile or be sick from. If Jakob could have perhaps seen the playful glint in the Captain's expression through the abrasive light, then he might have shared a wry smile.

"Do you understand, Jakob? Then congratulations, you have got the job. Do you have any questions? If you want to know whether you can see your wife or not, you can't. Besides, absence makes the heart grow fonder, does it not? And if you want to know when you start then I can tell you. There's no time like the present. Christian, would you please escort our guest to his quarters," the officer remarked, as if suddenly wanting to be rid of his charge.

"Yes sir. Heil Hitler!" the rough-voiced Private ejaculated whilst saluting. As he did so Jakob could not fail to notice how the soldier owned a stump, where his right hand should have been. His rifle was ornamental also.

"Yes, quite," Robert Fischer glibly replied, not even bothering to look up at the guard as he prodded the Jew out of the door with the barrel of his unloaded Karabiner Kar 98K.

*

Pinkish-grey clouds smeared themselves across the sky outside. Robert Fischer felt a slight draught, rather than the massaging rays of the sun, upon the back of his neck. More than one commentator had called the thirty-five year old 'devilishly handsome'. His cropped hair was light-brown, though it would grow fairer, like a child's, in the summer months. Robert was just short of six foot, broad shouldered and strong-jawed. His blue eyes could at once prove striking, and then prove unreadable - but they were always engaging. The officer's sun-kissed complexion had harvested the good life and his mouth could express either a sensuousness or sarcasm at the curl of a lip, depending on what mood possessed the changeable captain, or rather which mood Robert chose to possess. Such were his piratical good looks that Robert Fischer could have been one of the town's most famous, or infamous, womanisers even without the added attraction of his princely personal fortune.

Yet the officer's body of late had increasingly become a temple in ruins. His face was still symmetrical, but had grown a little rounder, plumper. He was a thirty-five year old who suffered from shortness of breath. But for the skill of his tailor Robert would have had a more pronounced stomach for all the world to see. His hair too this summer would recede as well as grow fair. But the retiring officer had no need to be fit for military duty. He was but a captain in name who had purchased a promotion to Superfluous Man. Bribes and favours cemented his privileged position and freedom from active duties. He had little desire to play a tragic role in the theatre of war. Often he fancied that he could be a real officer, whatever that meant, fighting at the front; he might have wished it now as he drew the curtains on another withering day and poured himself a large Napoleon brandy. But the mock-officer sometimes thought that he would have whisked himself off to battle not out of a love for his country, which he loved but scarcely recognised nowadays - but for the simple reason that it would be just something to do. Robert Wilhelm Fischer was a coward only in the respect of not being a hero.

Brandy after brandy was absorbed until oblivion hung over the horizon like the setting sun. It was an hour or so before the party. Nobody expected him to be sober for the occasion, so the least Robert could do was be accommodating and live up to his social circle's predictable expectations. Strauss waltzed in the background upon a gramophone as Robert killed time by carving sketches of faces and trees into his already scarred desk with his letter knife. I say his knife, but the initials "A.S" were engraved into the silver handle. The knife belonged to a Doctor Abraham Solomon. Robert had converted his surgery into a study when he had acquired the house a couple of years ago. *Am I nothing but a common thief?* Robert gently rubbed the initials under his thumb and told himself that all he felt was an engraved piece of silver; to feel anything else involved too much idle, discomforting conceit for the officer. It represented nothing.

"Am I to cut myself with this knife and wash the guilt from my hands in blood like some melodramatic character from a novel? Or am I to use this letter opener to open some letters?" the officer drunkenly, drolly posed. Robert briefly, wryly half-smiled to himself also as he opened some mail. Most of the post was dated months ago. *The mail service is functioning as proficiently as our army it seems.* There was a letter from his young cousin on the Eastern Front. Robert tossed the correspondence aside, before even opening it, and drained the remaining warming elixir from the bottle.

Ah, Napoleon Brandy. One of the few things French, along with Balzac and their natural inferiority towards us of course, that I can tolerate. I wonder if in fifty years' time there will be such a tonic as Hitlerian Brandy? I warrant it would be dark, dense, with a bitter and strangely fruity taste. The plebs would doubtless drink themselves stupid with it. Drown themselves.

Did you even invade Russia on the same day as the Corsican? Did History not tell you something? History tells us that history repeats itself. Now for that remark, Robert, you should reproach yourself. I do believe that statement had the air of a conclusion.

'I hold the world as but the world, a stage where every man must play a part, and mine is a sad one,'" the half-soused officer muttered to himself, smiling.

CHAPTER TWO

The party seemed to be full of life. In one corner slender nymphs dressed in tawny and silver provocative dresses – some wearing tiaras or bunny rabbit tails – were draped over paunchy officers, their flushed faces and smooth flesh glistening with sweat. Giddy giggles and snorts of laughter shot across the old church hall and were traded as if involved in a fire-fight. A girlish squeal sliced the air as the magistrate's daughter had her bottom rudely pinched; her response was to sit upon the offending soldier's lap and entwine her glitter covered arms around his neck and kiss him upon the tip of his nose. She didn't even know the daring assailant, but her sorority would have thought him handsome and he held an enviable rank. Two drunken, newly commissioned SS officers plucked a couple of decorative broad swords off the wall and were clumsily fencing with each other. No louder than the ringing in some of the party-goers' ears, Vivaldi was being played with no little accomplishment by a small chamber orchestra at the top of the hall. To make themselves heard however they switched to a piece of juvenilia by Wagner. The floor was sticky with spilt drinks, forming a sugary stench if a guest chose to notice it. Yet the rancid air of cronyism, oblique vanity and hypocrisy was just as pungent for the bored officer. Robert yawned, again.

"Am I keeping you awake, Captain Fischer?" remarked Anna Bremer, a middle-aged socialite whose colourful perfume proved far more overpowering for Robert than her beauty, charm or wit.

"I wish you would madam, I dearly wish you would."

"I hope that is the drink talking, Captain," the woman replied with an askance expression, her pencil eyebrows arching above her narrow eyes. Haughty.

"I can see a neck and lip on this bottle Mrs Bremer, but not a mouth nor tongue," Robert exclaimed whilst studying the bottle of wine with mock intent. A few of the men from the group, who did not smirk into their glasses, cupped their hands over their mouths.

"There is merit in Kant, Captain."

"Is there?"

"What a world it would be if all officers behaved like yourself, if you may permit me the poetic licence to call you an officer?"

"I am as much of an officer as you are a philosopher it seems, madam. Tell me, being a student of Kant, what do you think he would have said about the war?"

"Do you question the war effort, Captain? Do you hear this? Our brave captain here questions the war!" Anna Bremer said shrilly, looking to her circle for support.

"I question everything Mrs Bremer, especially your knowledge of Kant."

"And what am I to say to that?" Anna replied, again displaying a practiced look of supercilious disdain.

"Whereof one cannot speak, one should not speak," the officer riposted, quoting Kant.

Why am I here? – Robert Fischer asked himself. To forget myself, was the swift, automatic reply. This amusing role-playing is the arousing mistress to the frigid nag of my wife, boredom. You cannot be dejected all the time, as real and true as life seems when one peers through misery's black veil.

"Come, come, let's change the subject."

Robert neither knew the transparent fop who spoke up here - nor did he wish to get to know the priggish clod. He finished off his glass of wine so as to have a genuine excuse to free himself from the bleating elitist clique - consisting of lawyers, government officials and SS officers. A corner of his mouth was raised in a self-satisfied grin, or leer, when the predatory captain spotted Maria Schiller at the bar. She was talking to a young pock-marked corporal, yet her eyes often peered over his shoulder in search of worthier company.

"It is Nature's way. The wolves must devour the sheep," the Corporal steadfastly asserted, smoothing out his lank hair across his scalp with his palm as he did so, preening himself.

"But I thought Hitler was our shepherd," Robert announced, ghosting in upon the couple.

"Yes, I suppose he is. But our Fuhrer is the wolf's shepherd," the SS Corporal respectfully said to the Wehrmacht officer, forcing a smile.

"Wouldn't that make the Fuhrer a wolfherd though, Corporal?"

Maria announced – and then let out a burst of peach laughter, pleased that she had concocted up such a novel word, or clever comment. Robert's response to the SS lackey was to plaster upon his countenance some gargoyle half-smile, or sneer.

"Yes, I suppose it would, madam Maria. How clever of you."

"And should the wolf devour every sheep, Corporal?" Robert asked, amused rather than disgusted by the young soldier's fanaticism and ineptitude.

"He has no choice sir. It is Nature's way."

"And is it Nature's way that the wolf should die out for having no sheep left to devour? Or will he become a vegetarian, like your shepherd?"

"A good point sir," the corporal replied through a strained expression. Who had invited him to join their conversation anyway? – he posited beneath his breath. To speak of the Fuhrer so, in such an impertinent tone, was tantamount to blasphemy for the adolescent.

"I am sure that if Nature were here then he or she would be able to refute my argument," Robert said whilst patronisingly winking at the proud young soldier.

"Corporal, would you be a darling and give a message to my driver downstairs? Please tell him that I won't be in need of the car this evening."

"I am there already my lady. Heil Hitler, Captain."

Ignoring his young comrade's salute, Robert rudely looked over his shoulder to attract a waiter's attention.

"Heil Hitler, Captain," the youth repeated. His contorted

expression and high-pitched tone betrayed how riled he was by the captain's condescending attitude towards him.

"Must I crease my brow to show my contempt of you?" Robert laughingly put, but then glowered at the SS toad-eater, disgusted rather than amused now by his make-up.

"Oh Robert, don't tease him. He is not being serious, Simon. I do believe that the captain does not even know how to be serious. Now would you please be a dear and give the message to my driver? I do not want him to wait for me unnecessarily," Mrs Schiller asked whilst lightly touching the enamoured adolescent upon his pigeon chest with her fan.

"Yes, I understand. But I will return. I could not have hoped for such sympathetic and intelligent company this evening." The corporal's bow and clicking of his heels were as pronounced as his mediocrity, Robert judged. Not having a driver to find, for Maria had long since instructed him to go home, the green, dutiful, hormonal youth spent half the evening downstairs searching for him, desperately conscious of fulfilling his mission for the near aristocratic lady.

"Mrs Schiller," Robert remarked with a seductive light in his eyes, slightly bowing his head as if the couple were meeting for the first time.

Maria Schiller was the wife of the highly admired and highly promiscuous Marcus Schiller, German ambassador to Switzerland. The former actress was as intelligent as her genes and environment allowed, but yet one would forgive any deficiencies in Maria's character from her owning of an hourglass figure and almond eyes that a man could happily get lost in.

Robert paused and just gazed at the alluring woman again, admiring both her singular beauty and her sense of fashion. She was wearing a navy blue silk gown, cut low to reveal her pale, sculptured bosom. The sleeves and trim of the rustling dress were detailed with fine lace, the deep blue setting off Maria's white skin and sapphire eyes perfectly. A couple of shiny ringlets of blonde hair fell down over her classically beautiful face. Maria brushed them out of her eyes with her hands, which were gloved in matching navy blue silk, the material clinging to and emphasising her slender arms. Robert smiled appreciatively at her, as if Maria were a work of art. The lady coyly smiled back, revealingly, invitingly. The couple, who had slept together a few weeks ago, had not seen each other since that night. Both parties implicitly understood that the affair would remain casual. Yet Robert had rightly suspected that Maria wanted more from the relationship – and him. Hence he had refrained from answering her messages and attending a function that he knew Maria would be present at last week. As desperate and ripe as the subject was for Robert though, he believed that the seduction (or rather work of art) was only half complete.

"I missed you at the party on Thursday."

"I, I had to work," Robert replied, looking somewhat sheepish for once.

"You are a better philosopher than you are a liar, Captain," Maria said and smiled, whilst also conveying the piquet she had felt at him having ignored her messages.

"Do you know why I couldn't see you last week? Why I haven't called?" Robert remarked, lowering his head in shame almost to avoid the intimidating features of the bewitching woman.

"Why?"

"Because I'm frightened that this affair is not just an affair, yet I'm also scared that it might just remain so," the officer dramatically declared whilst simultaneously raising his head to reveal an intense, amorous expression. Smouldering love. Robert deliberately tried to talk in pained, yet impassioned prose. He knitted his brow and then softened his eyes so as to resemble an imploring child almost. For her part Maria's heart skipped a beat, shocked as she was to hear such an ardent confession from her lover, who was usually such a closed book. Maria's heart couldn't help but flutter also though, flattered and pleased as she was to have seduced the Byronic Captain. He too feels that this is not just another meaningless affair, Maria thought.

"I used to believe that hate was the opposite of love, Maria. Now I know that it is fear. All my life I have been cold, reserved, to keep myself safe. I believed that if I did not invest then I would not go bankrupt. But now I know that bankruptcy is caused, not prevented, by a lack of investment," he endearingly expressed. The woman's heart and eyes moistened with sympathy for Robert Fischer's devotion, and despair. The officer swallowed and tugged his finger at his collar, like a man remaining stoical in the face of a fever. He sketched sorrow, then frustration, and then desire in his features. The emotional officer then released the tension in his expression, rubbed his brow and shook his head. His vulnerability cemented his sincerity.

"No, I do not know how I feel," the officer said, as if to dismiss or annul the gravity of his recent confession. But Maria was confident of how her lover really felt and her soul trembled like the notes upon the yearning cello in the background, or so she wrote in her diary the day after.

"Then have faith in me that I know what you're feeling, because I've felt it, too. I know you Robert, we are the same. I have seen behind the act you put on for everyone. Let's leave. I suspect that you are as tired of this party as I am." Later on that evening Maria would also go on to declare, in relation to their social set, that they neither understood nor deserved the couple. Society was all so false. She could happily stay in the hotel room with her lover for eternity and never attend another party or see her infernal social circle again. She knew now how the poets felt when they wrote about love.

Robert at first squeezed the hand of Maria tightly, to convey his passion, but then he softly caressed it as she led him out of the bustling party. Maria's champagne-bubbled head swirled with emotion and anticipation, as if she were a character from one of the French romantic novels which she regularly devoured. Yet the glamorous woman was also brought back down to a more prosaic existence when the coarse and corpulent General Lars Haber accosted her officer and took him out of earshot, bluffly apologising to the lady for doing so.

"Robert, how are you, you villain?" he spluttered through his flabby jowls, clasping a fleshy hand around the Wehrmacht

Captain's shoulder.

"Fine, General. But Lars, more to the point, were you satisfied?" Robert remarked with a wink, all the time suppressing his natural dislike of the odious Nazi – and his feelings of distaste for having played the pimp for the General in setting him up with a former lover.

"The target was acquired," the General replied, winking back and guffawing. "I cannot thank you enough, Robert," he asserted, patting his Captain on the back with affection – with red wine and tobacco competing for primacy on his odorous breath.

"The reconnaissance was my pleasure, General," Robert said, to the reply of another Bavarian guffaw.

"You are a devil Robert, a veritable devil."

"Yet you must please excuse this devil, General. I am on another mission so to speak. Heil Hitler!"

"Heil Hitler!" General Haber solemnly saluted back, extinguishing his laughter. One should never laugh whilst mentioning the Fuhrer.

Robert freed himself from his superior before he had a chance to be amused by a vein throbbing in the general's neck as he passionately, drunkenly held the salute. Yet Robert couldn't fail to hear however, as he clasped Maria by the hand to lead her out, the following words of the highly influential senior officer.

"That Fischer is a fine fellow, a fine fellow – a good man in my book."

Robert Fischer at first sneered and then crimsoned – either in shame or anger at the statement.

CHAPTER THREE

Condensation dripped down the walls, like tears. An odour of damp fogged up the brooding air of the former wine cellar, now cell. A rusting steel bucket (toilet) and flaccid, fetid mattress sat next to each other on the stone floor. A dusty walnut bureau and chair belonging to Abraham Solomon's eldest son looked out of place in the squalid surroundings. Candles, a bowl of half eaten cereal, pens, paper and a tower of books rested upon the antique desk. There was nothing so dramatic or darkly poetic as a rat or spider crawling across the floor though, and Jakob appeared to be no unhappier for having to dwell in such a place, especially when he considered his former, dehumanising dormitory in which heads kissed feet nightly as men were packed in like sardines. Brother was all but forced to rob, bully and cheat brother.

The bones in his face were pronounced from starvation, his skin was grey like the protein deficient patches of his once black hair, which was now slightly longer than stubble length upon his scalp. Fifty years old. Decrepit. Weathered. Jakob smiled weakly to himself. He even imagined laughing to himself (*'man alone suffers so deeply that he had to invent laughter'* – *Nietzsche*). It struck the ascetic, whilst he was taking the time to try and delouse both his hair and mangy garb, that he had almost been rehearsing for this mode of existence for most of his life, desiring it even. The pensive Jew serenely closed his eyes, as if the sceptic were about to pray, to reveal a set of bruise-coloured eyelids. Even as a young teenager Jakob had been morbidly fascinated by how much solitude and privation he could endure, if his mind could make a heaven of hell. As a child many of his heroes had been recluses, scholars or misanthropic: Diogenes, Newton, Robinson Crusoe, Schopenhauer. In his mid-teens a studious Jakob would amuse himself by compiling and constantly revising the list of ten books and authors that he would take to a desert island. Shakespeare… Cicero… Voltaire… Epictetus…

And hadn't Jakob's desire for a hermetic life, free from the charades and cruelty of men, been a dream worth pursuing? Wars and tragedy still embroidered the tapestry of history. Now more than ever life was concerned with the survival of the fittest. Can we not forgive Levin for wryly smiling, having been proved right in his pessimism? *Man is Sin, or a disease. Life is still nasty, brutish and short.* Jakob had to smile to himself; calm must be preserved - they could only win if he joined their ranks. They could maul and soil his body, a body which is flawed and bestial by nature anyway, but they could not corrupt his mind, his true self. Jakob raised an eyebrow at a particularly large specimen of louse which he rubbed between his grubby forefinger and thumb.

The introspective prisoner's strange humour only faltered when his thoughts wandered onto his wife, Sara. He could not declare that he loved her in any sense of a grand passion or that she was his soul mate – but she was still his wife. It was an act of volition to try and remember her before the camp, but he had to picture Sara running her soft hands through her coal black tresses and fragrantly laughing at his stuffiness and dry humour. Sara had made Jakob promise that he would always remember her at her best – it was perhaps the only promise that she ever asked of her husband. He told himself that she was a practical woman and a survivor, but more so Jakob just formed a vague prayer to something – not God – that she would endure. The former philosophy tutor knew that it was an absurd, futile gesture, but Sara would be praying for a similar thing for him. The devout agnostic figured that it could do no harm. She would be invoking a more orthodox, though equally indifferent God, Levin construed. But work, rather than an abstract God, would save him from future maudlin and uncomfortable reveries he posited.

The authors of the books which lay in front of him were obscure, most of them (twelve of the twenty) Jakob had not even heard of, never mind read. But it would have been pointless he surmised to translate Milton and Coleridge – not because the German public knew such authors and their works (propaganda and time would be able to re-write history in that respect) but because their writings had already been sufficiently translated, some by a few of Jakob's former colleagues. Where were they now, he fleetingly imagined – German and Jew? But Levin quickly checked himself, pulling himself back from the emotional precipice. And so writers such as Sir Thomas Dicks and Andrew

Lampard were perched in front of the academic Jew. "Sir Thomas Dicks. The Sonnets", being on top of the pile, was the first book he opened and began to methodically work through. It felt good, homely, for Jakob to clasp a book in his hands again; he fondly held the cracked leather up to his nose and gently blew away the film of dust greying its tan cover.

Today is a good day.

CHAPTER FOUR

Robert returned to the house around midday, dissatisfied and fatigued but still attempting to grin to himself. He had spent the night with Maria in a suite at the Metternich Hotel. He recalled again with amusement how he had, in between bouts of ardent pleasure, cupped her face in his hands and ran his thumb gently across her cheek, confessing, "You're the only one, Maria, who can wipe the tears away from my eyes". Robert smirked. How the fond woman had not picked up upon the pastiche, the sarcasm in his voice when he had recited snippets of poetry to her was not surprising, though. That Robert had quoted from Faust to the woman, with a Mephistophelian smile upon his face, only enriched his sense of irony and ego.

"Tell me whether
We can have some peaceful time together,
Lie breast to breast and mingle soul to soul."

Maria had melted in his arms last night, as he too had permitted himself to surrender to her seductions for the evening. His confession had unleashed and deepened her passion and devotion. She was freer, wilder, (yet at the same time the woman felt safer) in her stimulating foreplay and lovemaking.

Never one for goodbyes, Robert had left a note for Maria by the bed, along with the champagne breakfast he had considerately ordered for her. It was not unduly difficult to compose something so heartfelt and romantic for the sultry creature that slept there so peacefully and prettily – the morning sun pouring in its amber rays through the curtains, transforming her demure face and slender legs into silk. But Robert was determined not to wake her; her voice, or conversation rather, would have disturbed the aesthetic. So too he had to remain sufficiently distant still and an enigma to Maria. If she thought that he had fallen in love with her too quickly it would ruin her novella and devalue her conquest, conversion, of the infamous Captain Fischer. "Treat 'em mean, keep 'em keen," the weary seducer joked as he entered his study.

Undoing his belt and the top button on his trousers, Robert slumped into his chair, conscious of the cliché sigh he emitted. Precious sleep was beckoning – oh, if only he could seduce Proserpine at will – but something caught the officer's eye. Neatly piled up in his 'In Tray' there rested several crisp sheets of paper filled with almost femininely fine handwriting. Only pride or a broken spirit could have produced such efficiency Robert pondered. He picked up the first couple of pages and began to read with as much interest as he could muster after the previous night's exertions.

"Thou dost of late chide how tardy I am
In plucking thy bloom when thou'rt in season.

When before I was akin to the ram
Who'd e'en charge the lion without reason.
But my love has grown since those sheepish ways
And thou'rt not a flower, but a fine wine –
Tasting sweetest when left open for days.
We should not rush, we should delay the time
When thy ripened fruit will enswell my head.
Besides, other sweet wines do I so taste,
Other flowers are in bloom 'pon my bed.
But sour not, thou wilt not go to waste.
For love, why should I not go out to dine?
Sober I'd be if I but drunk your wine."

The well-read German was as much impressed by the technical ability of his prisoner as a translator as he was by the wit of - Robert checked the name - Sir Thomas Dicks. Did this Jakob appreciate the wit? Could this Jew be as healthily amoral (immoral) as this sixteenth century sonneteer seemed? Robert then imagined Jakob in his cell translating and then polishing this gem, content and proud of himself. Who had had the more worthwhile episode last night, Jakob or himself? Robert read on, infected by a genuine curiosity from being a keen reader of poetry in his youth.

"Wake not to this anaemic moon tonight,
This November evening in darkness bright
Where the honeysuckle in the mud rots,
Trodden on by soldiers, careless as tots.

But sleep as deep as slumber darling wife,
Oblivious to Oblivion's life,
Who I see now. His Cyclopean-eye
Is peeping under a cloud on the sly.
He knows that I can see him, but acts still
As if a corpse were witness to his kill.
Oh I wish you were here my clement wife,
For Oblivion e'en might end his strife
In awe of such beauty, hope for our kind.
Yet keep out of his sight - and out of mind."

CHAPTER FIVE

One couldn't help but contrast the officer's slightly tanned, slightly red-nosed face with the death-mask pallor of Jakob's complexion. So too Robert's hair and contoured features shone brighter in the face of the Jew's gaunt expression and greasy hair. And as Robert's strong hands were soft and manicured, Jakob's were as coarse and blackened as his apparel. The senescent prisoner was a sight to breed both pity and contempt in equal measure, in differing eyes. It seemed as if life had whittled away at Levin for an eternity, yet the hand of pity or spite had failed to release him.

"That will be all Christian, thank you."

Christian, Jakob's jailor, snorted and left the officer and prisoner alone in the room together. Jakob stopped working and stood attentive to his imposing visitor. Robert was dressed in his uniform, but his jacket and collar were informally undone.

"Some red wine Jakob?" Robert amiably asked, having entered the room with a bottle of Burgundy and two glasses.

"No thank you Herr Captain," Jakob meekly answered, his head slightly bowed.

"Do you not drink?"

"I do not drink red wine."

There was deference, diffidence to Jakob's tone. Yet also Robert could begin to sense a certain matter-of-factness, or insolence, in the academic's air towards him. Robert had perhaps intended to behave amicably towards the unfortunate prisoner upon first arriving, but now his tone and attitude became laced with an atavistic playfulness and goading confidence. Both men were not without intellect - and ego.

"What are you working on?"

"One of a series of poems by Matthew Fry, a twentieth century poet. He adopts the character of a lovelorn, juvenile poet and both satirises and falls victim to the ideals of love and poetry."

"The earlier one falls victim to love, the better. For one can learn from the mistake. I look forward to reading it, Jakob. I couldn't help but be impressed by your initial translations. You're an intelligent man. If you were born a true German, life would have been very different for you, no? …I'm curious, do you blame a cruel or indifferent God for the position you're in?" Robert Fischer flippantly remarked whilst taking a swig of wine – but all the while never taking his eyes off the emaciated prisoner.

"No, I do not blame a cruel or indifferent God for the position I am in, Captain."

"You must resent the Nazis then?"

"No, not really," Jakob murmured.

"Forget this uniform Jakob, I know I try to. And not just because of its ill cut. Honesty cannot get you into any further trouble I warrant. I for one certainly detest the Nazis, but then again I find most men contemptible for one reason or another."

"I still do not resent the Nazis, Captain," Jakob replied, like a reticent child confessing a crime to his schoolmaster – or telling the truth in the face of a prospective punishment.

"Do you despise anyone then perchance?" the officer exclaimed, partly amused, partly intrigued.

"No."

Hatred was inefficient, illogical.

"Then you would forgive our munificent Fuhrer also?"

"If he was genuinely sorry for his crimes, then yes."

"I do believe you are the most Christian Jew that I have ever met, Jakob."

During the pause which followed Robert poured himself another glass of the blood-like vintage.

"I gather then that you do not resent me?"

"No," Jakob quietly remarked, shaking his head as he did so – either he wanted to stress the fact, or the sombre looking man did so as an expression of shaking off the doubts Levin had in regards to his negative reply.

Robert had planned to meet Jakob with good intentions, but there was something in the dry Jew's tone (not quite sanctimonious, not quite ironic; although Robert could not find the term, it existed) that slightly decentred the officer. The fish wasn't biting and the angler was running out of lures. And the officer sensed that it wasn't just fear which kept the prisoner in check, but rather a heightened state of self-possession.

"That's only because you don't know me. Would you rather not instinctively wish me damned rather than saved if I told you that it was my decision not to allow you to see you wife before your transfer?"

The prisoner was going to reply "Instinctively, maybe", but he merely calmly stated, "No".

"Are you usually this garrulous?" Robert half amused, half frustratingly replied.

Jakob was tempted to assert that the best person to ask and answer this would be his wife but the atrophied figure just humbly stood before his would-be tormentor, his drawn face and tired eyes looking down at the Captain's feet.

"Do you know what the meek inherit, Jakob? The existence of the punishment validates the punishment. If you turn the other cheek there are Romans who would strike that too. Pandora's Box has been opened. You should be angry, Jakob. You have every reason to resent people – me especially."

Robert paused and drank another glass of wine. If he were Jakob he would be inwardly enjoying himself right now. The usually nonchalant officer was displaying cheap shards of agitation, emotion and conviction. One had to be dislocated, ironic, that was the only way to combat and rise above the cesspool of life. But he had just briefly descended into that state of being which he deplored.

"Do you consider me a Nazi, Jakob?"

"No."

By now the gradient of Robert's drinking, pacing and blinking had steepened.

"You're uncommonly brave, stupid or wise Jakob. I haven't quite decided which yet. Let me ask you another question. It will be the last. I can see how you would rather return to exchanging sentences between books, than conversing with another human being. Do you think me Godless?"

The wizened prisoner raised his head to intently but gently examine the officer's hardened, anxious aspect. Jakob's own eyes were hazel brown, dark but once – so long ago now – warm.

"No," Jakob issued with confidence and sympathy.

"And I mistook thee for being intelligent," Robert exclaimed – and then sneered unpleasantly.

Before either Jakob or Robert could say anything else though they were interrupted by a returning Christian.

"I've been asked to tell you that your accountant is on the telephone Sir," Christian conveyed with a certain amount of awkwardness; he felt he was intruding upon the two men at a difficult moment. Bitterness could also be traced in his voice; he was such a dog's body to the officer that even the maids now felt that they could order him around in the hierarchy of the household. Christian was sweet on one of the servants though – and she seemed to be unmarried. But yet the soldier knew more than anyone how his affections wouldn't be returned. Nothing would or could become of his feelings - and he could only half blame his deformity.

Robert departed. Levin thought the officer somewhat erratic and gloomy.

The two often go together.

CHAPTER SIX

Time passes.

"I received a letter from Marcus yesterday, he has asked me to join him in Switzerland. You must understand that it is not because he fears the Russians. He says that he misses me. But I will miss you. Say that you feel the same way about me as I do about you and I will stay, Robert. But have I been flattering myself to think that I could prize a commitment from Robert Fischer? You are faithful to nothing, as you yourself have confessed. I do not even believe that you love yourself, let alone me. But I know you Robert and feel you are a good man. I must meet with you before I leave, if only to make you promise that you too will leave the country if and when the time comes. People may not publicly declare their fears about the Russians, but I will; I have heard the whispered talk. Dearest Robert, pray meet me tonight before I leave tomorrow. Give your answer to my messenger. Maria."

So ran the letter that Robert had just read. The already despondent captain was far from happy, his eyes impulsively began to burn holes into the name written at the bottom of the perfumed note, and he briefly expressed underneath his breath, quoting Hamlet,

"Now I could drink hot blood and do such bitter business as the day would quake to look upon it."

"Excuse me, Sir?" the young messenger hesitantly asked.

"You are to tell the lady that I was not at home. Inform Mrs Schiller that I was out making arrangements to sign up for the front. Do you understand?" Robert instructed whilst extracting a particularly large tip from his wallet. The herald was fearful enough of the affluent officer to honour his promise and earn his fee.

"Yes Sir," the young messenger dutifully replied, whilst greedily pocketing his bribe.

"That will be all, thank you."

"Yes Sir, thank you Sir. Good day to you."

Yes, it will be a good day, Robert decided after the messenger left. *How dare she!* He knew he was perturbed from his smarted pride at Maria choosing her husband over himself, but that was sufficient; his pride was his all. Robert was also singed from her insinuations and judgements that she felt she knew him and he was a good man. First some buffoon had deemed him a fine fellow and now this society whore had called him a 'good man'. *How insulting is it to be deemed fine and good by their base standards?* Robert here recalled the expression upon the strange Jew's face as he searched his eyes for a mirror to his soul. What Maria Schiller knew of him was but a part he played out for her; how dare she presume to know him, let alone judge him? He would prove them all wrong. He would ruin this beautiful soubrette's life. Why? Because he could. Robert's wound also smarted from the fact that he had underestimated this woman – and overestimated the devotion she carried in her heart for him. Or had she reached her melodramatic conclusions using the same sources from which she gleaned all her other perceptions? From delusional romance novels, cliché-ridden magazine articles and women's table talk.

"If your greatest wish is to have some melodrama in your life, then you shall have it. If saving your captain will make you happy, then he will be saved," Robert muttered with an almost diabolical expression on his flushed face.

The spurned lover, as petulant and adamantine as Achilles, proceeded to write, at the pace of his vengeful beating heart, a letter to Herr Schiller. It disclosed a confession concerning one of Maria's past affairs. She had told her present lover about her first adulterous affair a month or so ago. The affair had been as brief as it had been anti-climactic. Three years ago Maria had spent the night with a hotel concierge after she had correctly suspected her husband of having an affair. After the initial shock Maria had, quite rightly, felt nothing but the desire for revenge. The most challenging part for Robert now, however, consisted of conjuring a reason as to why a person, a past lover, would compose such a letter? In the end the devotee of Stendhal and Turgenev made up the plot device that Oliver (the concierge) was now fighting on the Eastern Front, and he wished to clear his conscience of his sins before he died. Robert really was quite proud and touched by his own private's eloquence. A small payment to the mail service could make the letter appear to have been sent from the Front – and also make it reach its destination around the same time as Maria would reach Switzerland. Yes Robert indulged in picturing the scene of Marcus Schiller's hypocritical indignation and dejection – and he even amusingly fancied the shallow despair and denials of Maria. But just that he had been the author of such innovative unpleasantness was satisfaction enough for our German Pechorin.

The Schiller marriage was already but a farce of conjugal bliss. To redeem the slight suffered at the hands of his unfaithful and ungrateful mistress, Maria had to pay in a cost innumerable. Not content with the love, amusement and ecstasy he had inspired in her, Robert would now instil in Maria that which made a mockery, a living-hell, of his paltry life – guilt.

It had been some time since the morose Robert had felt this enlivened or purposeful. Although the happy couple were far from worthy enemies, they were enemies nevertheless. The powers to pardon, condemn and create were his to summon at will. Jakob was but a translator of poetry; here Robert was composing a living, breathing narrative. Anything which brought this much joy to a person must be justifiable, the officer thought, half-jokingly, to himself.

CHAPTER SEVEN

The polished sunlight proliferated through the curtains of the apartment's drawing room. Maria fanned her face with her elegant hand and long, tapering fingers as she began to perspire and feel a little flushed. She paced around the room, subtly repositioning various porcelain figurines and checking herself in one of the many mirrors upon the walls, before settling upon a heavily cushioned chaise lounge. As well as being in two minds as to whether Robert would now come or not, the woman was in a quandary as to the following: Maria wanted to give the impression that she had been crying, but at the same time did not wish to spoil her make-up. The sensible lover suitably wished to be at her most memorable for what could be her final encounter with the only man who had ever truly understood and satisfied her. Indeed if she looked and acted alluring enough then Robert might hesitate in his decision to leave for the death-sentence of the East. He could still join her in Switzerland and they could continue to see each other. Although it was now mid-afternoon Maria was still wearing her pearly, satin dressing gown, the belt of which clasped her slim waist to enhance the lines of her pristine figure. Her lips were constantly moistened and her bosom, immodest underneath her enticing gown, heaved succulently. Her glossy and full-bodied hair, free from the constraints of pins, was naturally fragrant and cascaded over her shoulders, a beautiful compliment and relation to the sunlight shimmering through the window. Maria fingered the pearl necklace he had given her, remembering the passion-filled evening in which she had done so. The woman smiled, dreamily, mournfully – as if the war had already taken him.

Robert was polite and informal with the lady's staff, even sharing a joke with one of the maids, but as he was just about to enter the drawing room the officer suitably wore a look of death and distraction on his countenance. It was only to be somewhat expected that Maria should have fluffed the lines and pose that she had rehearsed when, hair uncharacteristically unkempt, Robert made his entrance.

"Have you come from home?" Maria anxiously asked, fearing that she would now have to express those things included in the letter in person.

"No. I have been out for most of the day. There is something that I must tell you Maria. I still cannot quite believe it myself," he remarked, forcing a smile. Robert fondly gazed at Maria as if entranced by her beauty. Or he seemed preoccupied, troubled. The messenger had not been mistaken. The awkward silence was broken by Oscar the spaniel scampering over to the officer and yapping with excitement. Oscar's taking to her lover had also been the seal of Maria's taking to him all those weeks ago. For a split second or two, whilst affectionately stroking Oscar behind the ear and playing with the dog, Robert almost forgot his part. But yet during this brief pause Maria became even more contorted, yet limp with a feminine dread.

"I'm glad you're here. I have something important to say to you also, Robert," the lady uttered, trying to mine the words from her dry mouth in a voice unsure of itself. Robert ran his hand through his hair while Maria nervously bit her bottom lip.

"Why did you ask if I had come from home?"

"I sent you a note today to ask for you to come and see me."

"And I'm glad I have. You look beautiful Maria, but then you always do. I cannot approve of you spending the day in bed though so to speak, or at least without me. One of us wasting our lives is more than enough."

Maria inhaled and altered her expression, as if she were about to make a confession, but in one practised movement the vulnerable soldier knelt before the woman and clasped her hand, supplicating her as if she were an empress.

"You are right about me Maria, you always have been. My life has been but a deferment of living. I've gone over the words a thousand times in my head, but still I don't know how to tell you this. Now I know what people mean when they say that they have their hearts in their mouths. If I am to love you, and you love me, I must respect myself." Robert here briefly paused to absorb the awesome pity, love and admiration that the former actress felt for her captain. "The most insane thing I've ever done in my life is also that which feels most right. I suspect that the war will end within a year. If I do not come back a dead man, I will at least come back a new man." (Robert here endearingly affected an attempted smile). "No, I should not joke. I have signed up for the Front. I know that it might seem the wrong time to ask, but will you marry me Maria? Give me something worth fighting for, a light at the end of the tunnel."

A hundred teeming thoughts and sensations vied for sovereignty behind Maria's fine blue eyes as the seducer's performance washed over her; the electronic impulses of agony and ecstasy crackled in the woman's quaint brain. He loved her. How cruel fate was; only now, when they were about to be parted, did she fully realise how they were meant to be together. It was as though someone was playing a heartless prank upon the lovers. Should she tell him of her husband's letter? This new life of a new openness between them must begin with a lie. She felt guilty. But Maria did not have the heart – for it would break his – to tell him right now. But surely she would have to. Should she divorce her husband immediately, for how could she entertain a re-conciliation with Marcus, loving Robert so? But what if she divorced Marcus and Robert did not come back from the Front? She would have nothing, no one. At the back of her mind the woman knew the material truth that it was better to be melancholy than impoverished. Oh that the earth could have swallowed the poor would-be aristocrat up. Maria sniffled and tried to suppress the tears, but she was a woman.

The cynical romantic read the internal despair and crisis in his subject's face, her tears cutting scars through her make-up. Never had Maria looked so comical, pathetic, tragic, beautiful and interesting, he would later muse. Robert then rested his head upon her soft lap, partly to hide his lawyer-like smirk. She took his scalp in her hands and maternally stroked his hair. It was at this point that Robert realised that he wanted now to make love to Maria – and make love to the woman so she would never forget; partly out of gratitude perhaps for the amusement and pleasure she had given him over the last month or so.

"If only you would have said something before. I will marry you, but you cannot sign up for the Front. Please do not do it for my sake. I love you now for the man that you are, not for the man that you can or will be. I don't want to change you."

"I have signed up for myself also. And I can assure you that I have every intention of coming back, if you'll have me."

"No, you don't understand. I received a letter from Marcus. He wants me to join him in Switzerland, as soon as possible."

The soldier appeared thunder-struck by the news, his mouth agape. The spurned lover had to swallow, to catch his breath, before speaking.

"Does he desire a re-conciliation?" Out of the corner of her eye Maria could see Robert tensely grip one of the cushions on the sofa as he asked the searching question.

"I do not know, probably. But I couldn't care less about Marcus now."

"No, it's best that I go. He is your husband and I cannot guarantee I will return. I should leave," Robert selflessly announced, torture and sadness etched in his expression, kissing Maria upon the forehead as he got up.

"No, please, don't go. Stay with me for one more night – and then forever after that. You can still write to me and when the war is over I can get a divorce. Every day I'll pray for your return," Maria pleaded, feverishly clasping Robert's large hand.

"You mean that? You'll wait for me? You really love me?"

"I love you so much that there will be nothing left of myself soon. More now than ever, I will not be able to stop thinking about you. I may be married to him, but I will be faithful to you, Robert. I promise," the emotional woman lovingly exclaimed, almost taken back by her own eloquence and force of feeling.

Maybe they were even genuine tears in his eyes as the seducer, feigning calm rapture, knelt down before Maria again and amorously gazed up at her. The expression he received in return was one of a love unbridled, deep and slavish. Yet, despite transcending the experience of the word 'love' for Maria, she would return to her husband; he willed it that way. But Maria was not now the enemy as the sensualist slipped his warm hand through the slip in her dressing gown, supplely kissed her upon the mouth and made love to her slowly, deliberately, better.

*

An evening breeze billowed out the curtain and cooled his sticky skin. Robert showered, dressed and made his way out of the apartment like a thief in the night. Maria slept on, her arm draped over a pillow, which she may or may not have mistaken for the chest of her lover. Robert had hoped to leave Maria with a final, poetic declaration of love but, unable to compose anything worthy of matching his poetic performance beforehand, he shrugged and abandoned the idea.

"Happiness is victory," he triumphantly and jauntily expressed to himself out loud, as he made his way down the deserted street. With his mind still buzzing with a sense of play Robert made a mental note to remind himself to write a letter to Maria in a month's time or so. It would be from a fictional intimate comrade of the gallant captain, containing news of his death. *I shall die both heroically and needlessly of course. This friend, a Heinrich perhaps, might even report that I died with Maria's name upon my lips. Yes, a nice touch. Such has been our romantic affair, and the love she bears, the woman might even remain faithful to my memory for more than a week.* With the tone and content of the letter fresh upon his mind, Robert duly composed it upon returning home, leaving a note to his secretary as to the instructions and date regarding its postage.

The next day, in a mood coloured with both grief and optimism concerning her new-found love, Maria Schiller left Germany to join her prosaic husband in Switzerland. During the train journey she calculated that Robert was as much as three times as wealthy as her husband, but that was not the reason why she loved and was attracted to her Captain. She arrived before the letter, but the outcome would have been the same should it have been the other way around. For neither the first nor last time in his life Marcus Schiller struck his wife. At a time when Maria should have been dazzling her new set with her urban style and Saxon looks she remained in her room, nursing a nasty bruise and depression. Life grew unfair for Maria and she soon became resentful of her husband and society. She felt trapped, dependent. Her beauty waned, like her so recently blooming heart. The lively, coquettish light that previously flashed in her eyes began to shine internally, reflecting upon the buried treasure of her and her captain's love. As she had helped to save him, so too Maria daily hoped and sighed that Robert would come and rescue her from the false, loveless world that she was living, dying, in. Love conquers all. Yet the consoling feelings derived from the reality and dream of their affair was, on many days, overshadowed by waves of regret. Let the sky fall upon her, but let her turn back the clock. Regret is a cancer. Maria's grief grew into a fully-fledged fever – even the local spring waters could not cure her. Eventually though the woman recovered from her "nervous disorder", but not two days afterwards she was physically sick again upon receiving the touching and awful letter from the good Heinrich Ballack, a comrade of Robert's. A piece of her died with the news. For month upon month a consuming dejection haunted the lady's private and public face like an unflattering shadow. Her husband did not even try to conceal the fact that he had a mistress, albeit he threatened his wife with abandonment should she try to take a lover again. Such was her torment that only wine and delusional recollections of her Captain soothed, but also aggravated, the woman's sorrows. Maria Schiller even remained faithful to Robert's memory for two whole years before taking another lover – Didier, a Nantes plumber.

CHAPTER EIGHT

Christian Boar was now beyond merely spitting in what little food he decided to serve to his parasitic prisoner. For the past week or so the former member of the Communist Party had amused himself by urinating in the Jew's meals and imagining the animal being so debased as to consume the disgusting food. Jakob was almost daily wasting away – a discoloured lead soldier, its enamel fading. Rusting. The skeletal lines of his chest and back were becoming sharper and his face increasing resembled a skull.

The brawny guard placed the piss-soaked bread and rancid butter upon the desk.

"Everything all right, uncle?" Christian issued in an overtly sarcastic tone.

An exhausted Jakob responded with silence and inertia. Christian resented this; he resented having to prepare the zhid's meals – this 'life unworthy of life' – and then going to the trouble to spoil them (frequently urinating on his own feet and ankles in the downstairs toilet as he performed the unseemly act). The soldier resented feeling like the Jew's secretary, looking after him and ferrying his work up to the captain's office each day. Even when reduced to a dog this Jew thought himself superior to the German, acting as if he didn't exist. The former would-be sergeant resented losing his hand in the war (Christian reported to people that he had his hand shot through during a fire fight in Krakow, but in truth he had fallen over in the curb one drunken evening in Poland and a car had crushed all the bones in it). And now even that whore of a domestic servant upstairs had stared at him the other day as if he were some kind of monster, or half a man.

The bullish son of a miller was tempted to rip up or spoil some of the sheets of airy-fairy poetry that rested on Jakob's desk, but Christian feared that it might eventually get back to his saturnine captain. He reckoned that the educated officer liked this Jew, if only for being a source of amusement and curiosity for the rich, spoilt dandy. When he had visited him that one time the captain had even offered the prisoner some wine and was friendly towards him. So too the captain had enquired about the welfare of the mangy zhid afterwards. When Christian had replied, "He is vermin, that is all you can say about him," the captain had drily countered, "Vermin, unlike perhaps your good self, Private, cannot translate poetry". But Robert had only visited the prisoner that single time and he probably only appreciated the Jew for the poetry which the mime of a real officer read with visible pleasure before sending it off to the Ministry of Propaganda.

When Christian departed with his customary grunt cum snigger, Jakob returned to his desk from the corner of the room, where he meekly stood whenever his keeper entered. Although his expression did not betray his agony, Jakob was being tortured by a clanging headache, as if some of the creases of his brain were being beaten closer together and his skull was compressing in on itself. The pain hammered like a gavel upon a block behind his pupils. He couldn't work, concentrate. The air, thick with the stench of his own liquid stools, nauseated him. The mind cannot make a place of its own, divorce itself from the body. Until now Jakob had told himself that his body could degenerate, that it wasn't him – that there was sufficient dualism in his philosophy. But his mind was but an organ, prone to decay and corruption. There is no transcendent self, Spirit. The body envelops and feeds the mind, bending it to the will of circadian desires and biologically pre-programmed impulses. His will was not his own, in so many ways, Jakob tiredly lamented. Sooner or later would he not gobble up his poisoned food like some savage? Appetite, a base desperation, would overpower the demands of his palate and pride.

Sleep was the only salvation from his gnawing hunger and lashing migraine. Jakob would even risk punishment for falling behind in his work in exchange for that blissful balm, realm. As Jakob curled up upon his putrid, damp mattress he suddenly recalled fragments of a darkly comic prose poem that he had composed about sleep when not twenty years old.

The travel had been arranged by the University. The three prize-winners sat in a freshly white-washed waiting room. It looked like a dentist's reception area, or mental asylum. Such was their desire to pick up their prizes that all three of the students deferred the tour until sometime later.

After all, Heaven wasn't going anywhere.

Midas, being the eldest of the three candidates, was the first to be called in to collect his prize.

And Midas' wish became his curse. Before he had even a chance to begin his acceptance speech, the Gods, like a pack of teacher-less school children, commenced to titter and smirk. And their sniggers, at first blanked out by the blinding glister of gold, continued to buzz in Midas' ears until his tragic, comic, death.

A quick check of their birthdays between the two remaining prize-winners revealed that Alexander was the next in line. The receptionist, a beautiful but officious Seraph, escorted the accomplished young man in. Ambitiously – and proudly – Alexander requested that everything he ever willed should be gratified. There was a slight murmur and discussion between a few of the lower Scribes in the Council but, after a minor blood (ichor) transfusion, Alexander was granted his great prize. But every desire that Alexander had after leaving Heaven was not only gratified, it was also negated. He felt perennially unsatisfied. Something was always missing. Even when Alexander saw the breadth of his domain he wept, for there were no more worlds left to conquer. The Gods could hardly breathe for their laughter - and their tears of joy were cruelly mixed with the remarkable young man's tears of grief upon his sodden map that dark and lonely night. His kingdom would also not outlive him.

It was far from easy for the Gods to keep a straight face, but when the final candidate was ushered into the great hall they miraculously regained their sage, austere composure.

"Congratulations, child."

Jakob offered them a look and pursed his lips to express that he was un-

amused at being patronised so by the Gods.

Jakob heard the sound of a falling goblet and some wine splash upon the floor. The solemn countenance of what seemed to be the principle legislative God – his silvery-grey beard offsetting his snow-white tunic – became a little stern or severe even. Realising how his demeanour must have appeared though, the Chancellor quickly softened his aspect and his tone became sympathetic, yet politic.

"I am sorry Jakob, but your wish to be blessed with the sense of humour of the Gods is the one thing that we cannot grant. Just say the word though and we will rightly bestow upon you any other blessing your heart desires, Riches, Artistic gifts, Knowledge, Power."

Disappointed, but far from distraught, the pessimistic student faltered not and here asked for the gift of sleep. As it was granted a chorus of goading laughter skewered the air like fireworks in the prize winner's direction but Jakob, as easy as if he were clicking his fingers, escaped their mockery by dipping his head into the warm waters of slumber.

CHAPTER NINE

"Your change, Sir," the oleaginous shop owner remarked, smiling as if he had just swallowed a coat hanger, as Robert finished purchasing a plain white shirt.

"Thank you," the officer replied, a little uncomfortable and irritated by the obsequious tailor's manner.

"Excellent choice, Sir. You are fortunate. It was the last one of its design in the shop."

"Yes, you have mentioned that once or twice already. Please, I have already bought it. There's no need – and you do not have the stock – for me to buy another."

"I am only trying to be friendly, Sir," the middle-aged salesman replied, rolling his eyes and now turning his nose up at the ill-mannered officer. The man thought to himself how the army was the cause of his country's ruin, rather than its salvation.

"No, you are just trying."

"Would you like it if I said nothing then, Sir?" the slightly camp owner waspishly countered – his tone polite and sarcastic in equal measure.

"You actually might be surprised at how successful that sales technique might prove. Good day."

"With respect, Sir, I think I'll keep appealing to a customer's sense of vanity if it's all the same to you," the now sour faced man remarked, smoothing his greasy hair behind his ears and pressing his lips together in a thin, artificial smile.

"With slightly less respect I should confess that this shopping spree was borne from boredom rather than vanity."

The officer's contempt for himself – and the world around him – fed off each other.

Robert, unshaven and even more disheartened by it all than usual, took the weight off his feet and sat upon a bench in the town square. The air was refreshingly crisp, helping the officer wake up from the previous evening's hangover. A brace of silver birch trees scented the breeze and flanked the nonchalant looking officer. He scratched tiny flecks of mud from his freshly polished black boots. Robert swiftly buried his head in his newspaper when he spotted a flock of women - widows, wives and vapid socialites who had made a play for him over the past month. Was he a piece of meat to them, as they were to him?

Robert also covertly spotted from across the street another family about to depart, migrate west. The Russians would be coming from the east. He tried not to form any judgements regarding the burgeoning exodus, he was neither angry nor sympathetic with them; it existed, like the war. Any other thoughts concerning the war were inherent with such subjectivity, irony, that Robert was averse to entertain them (*'You say that a good cause justifies even war? I say unto you; it is a good war which justifies any cause'* - *Nietzsche*). Irony, that double-edged sword which can turn lead into gold, but more often gold into lead, can annul the essence of everything except its own nothingness. The officer would rather hold no opinion than a half informed one. Meaning was the Philosopher's Stone to which Robert had long since given up the search. But that there was comedy in everything, therein was the tragedy. If everything was meaningless, so was he. His was a 'life unworthy of life' the brooding officer had morosely joked one evening last week.

But Robert let the muddy stream of life flow over him and his marble heart. Like coloured notes upon a page, a party of birds flew across the sky; the flutter of their wings and boisterous warbling disarmed the caustic officer of any enmity or envy he might have felt for the ragged herds of selfish good people who trundled by.

A few of the birds – sparrows and starlings – landed near Robert's feet, foraging for crumbs which had been dropped around the bench. The officer would have enjoyed nothing better now than to have fed the birds himself, but he glanced down the street and abandoned the idea after observing the length of the queue snaking out of the grocery store. Robert was conscious that he was choosing to immerse himself somewhat in this escapist's retreat of being a poet or fond, foolish old man, but he nevertheless continued to do so with a look of pleasant repose upon his face.

A mother was gazing into a shop window, at a pair of shoes. If she could have witnessed her two boys were up to she might have chastised them, if only on the grounds that her cherubs were getting their hands dirty as they picked up stones. The children could have been no older than twelve but they had the devil and such triumphant joy in their eyes as they ran and pelted the society of birds with bullet-sized missiles. Robert felt the first chunk of gravel strike his boot. What was he to do? Create a scene and reproach a couple of innocent children for enjoying themselves? All the birds seemed to escape the short-lived attack anyway, except one. A jagged pebble ricocheted off the soldier's sole and struck an adolescent starling. The shock, never mind the blow itself, might have killed the creature but yet Robert was thankful when he saw the bird wing its way up to the protection of the expansive sky and then the town's cathedral.

Along with some of his brothers and sisters the starling perched himself upon the statue of Christ, his arms spread-eagled in a welcoming rather than crucifixion pose, which was situated high up in an alcove of the looming structure. The figure was besmirched with feathers and excrement; the parishioner who generously used to maintain the statue was now a parishioner who used to be – his blood browning the sands somewhere in North Africa. Even the marks where he used to daub the figure's hands with red paint were indistinguishable. Yet, as discoloured and worn a figure as it now was, compared to its former glory, it still possessed those eyes – those noble and intimate eyes that followed one around the square as a great portrait's eyes can follow you around a room. Robert felt now that those eyes were looking down upon no one but him, like a disappointed father gazing upon his spiteful and sorry child. Life and love – distinct yet also inseparable – gazed down upon him. Words echoed through Robert, recalled from his childhood and idealistic youth; sometimes they glowed, bright – but they also scorched.

"Jesus Christ is the same yesterday, today, and forever... The light shines in the darkness... Fight the good fight... If you want to come with me you must forget yourself and take up the cross every day... Whoever wants to save his own life will lose it, but whoever loses his own life for my sake will save it... To be controlled by human nature results in death and life; to be controlled by Spirit, however, results in life and peace."

Robert felt the old weight rise up again and rest upon his shoulders, like a yoke. The colour drained and flushed up in his face alternately. Tears of despair and devotion welled in his blue eyes, but fell not. His breathing became irregular and, for the life of him, Robert could not swallow. He remembered Rebecca again, his fiancée. He had loved her. She had renewed his faith in goodness, God. Yet he had also mistreated her. *Why, if you are perfect, did you create such an imperfect world? An indifferent God is a heartless one. Why should I submit to you or have faith in you? But you – you are not!*

The telemetry between the pained officer and his reverie was finally interrupted by the vibration and rumble of a passing, hulking tank. A swastika, on a flag pointing up from the metallic behemoth, also impaired his view and brought Robert back to his senses. He had to laugh at the fantasist who mistook accident for fate – and too much coffee for a revelation. A comforting and superior sense of irony and sarcasm returned. Sentiment is something that is found at the bottom of a wine glass, he joked to himself. Robert glanced around to check if anyone had just witnessed his scene and conceited carry-on. He then straightened his uniform and commenced to return home.

Slightly numb with a chill and still reeling from his reverie upon the bench, Robert walked on. Sweat glazed a waxy complexion. He nervously bit upon the inside of his mouth – and noticed not when he broke the skin. Although far from scenic, Robert decided to take the most expedient way back to the house. The RAF had left its mark on most streets. Slate grey tenements buildings, cobwebbed with criss-crossing clothes lines, blocked out the sun and fresh air. A healthy glow finally returned to his cheeks and aspect when Robert reflected upon the fear and suspicion that his presence was inspiring in the community. The gossip of viper-tongued washerwomen eerily came to a stop as the powerfully framed officer passed them by – as did the cackles from a toothy chimpanzee hanging his head out the window and chatting to his witless cockroach of a neighbour. A smoking pit-bull of a man marking his territory – and a swarthy dominant bull holding court in a tenement doorway – both averted their glances when the Wehrmacht Captain caught their eyes. His contempt for Nietzsche's Man returned – and Robert told himself that everything was right with the world again. Yet still the despairing officer felt sick at heart.

Contempt dramatically turned to pity when Robert encountered a tramp lying at the end of the street. Under his mud-coloured rags and blood-caked beard he must have been about fifty. He was dead to the world, but for his abrasive snoring which was amplified through his bushy nostrils. A pungent smell of beer and ordure emanated from the prostrate figure.

The vagrant suddenly stirred however as Robert stood over him. Confusion and terror vied for ascendancy in his blood-shot eyes as he took in the strange-looking officer. Was he going to be arrested? He tried to speak but instead the tramp coughed up a smattering of blood and, with a lifetime of tobacco and schnapps behind him, the half-inebriated widower wheezed with consumption.

Without a word the officer extracted what money he had in his pocket and placed it into the beggar's rough hand. So too Fischer placed his new shirt beside the bewildered man. Robert later imagined how comical the careworn vagrant would look in the garment, but that was not the reason why he gave it to him.

Increasingly troubled, Robert continued to walk home, his feet as leaden as his heart. Feelings of guilt stalked him like a shadow. Robert finally wept, overcome with emotion – despair, contrition. Tears cleanse the soul. Revelation lashed down his spine like lightning, albeit please do not place too much literal significance in the term 'Revelation'. It was as if Robert remembered something that he had always known. God had been in his life before Rebecca even. If He wasn't, she would have never fallen in love with him. The Dionysian chants of his ego which coiled around the cynic's ear were displaced by the simple authoritative wisdom of the Gospels. Long had Robert's conscience been like a child trapped beneath the ice; how the devout sceptic and epicurean had laughed to himself in the past upon witnessing the futility of the asphyxiating child clamouring on the frozen lake or clawing with desperation for a break in the ice. Yet was there not something admirable, as well as comical, in this child's absurd defiance and mission to breathe? And now the glass had finally cracked. The ground was cut out from beneath him like a prisoner on the gallows. Robert's submission brought a sense of deliverance – enlightenment. Faith, goodness, are muscles which need to be exercised. Admitting to his burthen, it was relieved a little. His conscience felt as real as his sin. Thankfully the end of the street was deserted, for the weeping officer looked somewhat ridiculous, like someone who is about to yawn or sneeze. Tears glistened like pearls upon a changed countenance.

The effulgent afternoon sun shone through the thinning clouds again – warming the breeze – and lighted Robert's way home.

CHAPTER TEN

Around the same time that day when Robert was shopping, Christian Boar was alleviating his time in the tavern. It was not exclusively an establishment for soldiers but, this mid-afternoon, it appeared to be solely occupied by various low ranking officers, ex-soldiers and fellow Christians; perhaps they were the only folk with the sufficient funds, time and sorrows to drown. Christian and his comrade Wolfgang, a self-proclaimed ex-soldier and veteran Party member, were talking together in a booth.

"If nothing else, the efficiency and the organisation of the operation must be admired," Wolfgang reiterated, licking foam from the frothy beer off his lips.

"I would save the Reich the bother of one of them, put a bullet through the skull of that rat I have had to be nurse maid to. If nothing else, Germany will no longer be blighted by their kind at the end of the war, if what you say is true. It would just be like putting down a mangy dog. The only argument against putting a bullet through his head is that it would be a merciful death," Christian exclaimed through gritted teeth, screwing up his face in resentment to impress upon his elder, his similar fanatical hatred and sense of national socialist justice.

The smug grin that Wolfgang gave as his initial reply almost consumed the whole of his leathery pate. He was smiling in superiority to the pliable yokel who he believed he had successfully converted to his philosophy (will to power, mixed with the racial ideology of Nazism). Wolfgang Nerlinger was now fifty-five years old. He was a short, bull-necked man with a hook shaped nose and eyebrows that would have met in the middle but for his trimming of them with a razor blade. The parting of his dyed black hair yearned to cover the whole of his scalp. His eyes were two slits, expressionless unless burning with fury or schemes. Born to a well-to-do lower middle-class family, Wolfgang's childhood was trauma free and he was more of a bully than bullied. The Great War humbled him not, serving as he did, far from the front as a floor manager in an armament's factory in Bremen for most of the conflict. Wolfgang however felt as bitterly betrayed as any soldier on the Western Front when a fraudulent government betrayed his country and surrendered to the enemy. Due to the surrender, Wolfgang lost his job and the small sense of self-importance he derived from his bureaucratic power as an officious floor-manager. The Treaty of Versailles only rubbed salt in the wound for the proud German. He blamed the nation's crippled economy on the reparations demanded by the French. Wolfgang was unemployed for long periods – refusing work which he felt was beneath him. For the most part he lived off the inheritance that he came into after his father died. He wallowed in self-pity and prejudice, particularly riled by the Jews who cavorted with the sluttish German girls on the street below his squalid apartment. He drank, but also read a lot. Wolfgang even considered himself to be a somewhat amateur philosopher. Finding nihilism unfulfilling, Communism illogical, and other philosophies too abstract to follow, the Nazi Party saved and resurrected him. The timing of his call to the Party was also perfect. Wolfgang had fallen in love with one Erin Wesse, the pretty daughter of his landlord, a year before he fell under the spell of Hitler and the Nazi Party. At first his love was unrequited, and then spurned; finally she was unfaithful and Wolfgang woke up to reality, resentment. The friendless bachelor soon became married to the Party and cause, bringing purpose and belonging to a previously unemployed existence. Wolfgang was akin to a Dickensian character almost. His swollen blood-red gums housed a set of small, sharp yellow teeth; he was seldom seen without his worn, cracked black leather overcoat which he partly wore in imitation of the Gestapo. The arthritic man, who the children in his building called 'the codger', possessed a slight limp which he sometimes exaggerated to gain sympathy and attention – explaining the rheumatism away from receiving a wound at Verdun. The well-read anti-Semite owned a catchphrase if you like, 'There is no evil that I have not yet considered', which he borrowed from Goethe.

"More than mercy Christian, serve the Jew justice. Are you still spitting in his food in front of him? I bet the swine still laps it up. The creatures are feral. I used to have a Jew on my block that drank fresh chicken blood."

"No, he hasn't eaten for days."

"Has your captain visited him anymore?"

"No. I just think he went there to torment him that once."

"Everyone should have his own personal Jew to torment, a scapegoat. Restraint from one's instincts can only be suppressed so much. Our race should conquer and enslave Europe simply because it can. But I imagine that Jew torments you just as much as you torment him, eh?"

Wolfgang took a healthy swig of his beer, all the time surveying the reaction of his drinking companion. He happily saw Christian's face scrunch up and his eyes narrow.

"You have no idea how much I despise that pissing ant, having to clean out his toilet and tend to him. He just stands there like a dumb statue whenever I enter the room. He won't even look me in the eye."

Christian was here going to add that he was not the freak the Jew was, but he remembered his hand. Albeit not as self-conscious as he used to be about his amputation, it was still a source of embarrassment, misery and anger to Christian. He tried to block it out of his mind. Using only his right arm had become habitual and there were enough other casualties of war nowadays for him not to stand out so much. Christian was not the only one drawing awkward, covert glances from people who knew nothing of what war was really like. But still the former tractor mechanic felt an itch where his left hand had been, but it was now second nature to ignore it.

Wolfgang was bored. He tapped his foot, drank his beer and

listened to the unintentional humour generated by his friend. For the past few days the anti-Semite had been holed up in his apartment. In spite of the propaganda the news was still dispiriting. Germany was no longer winning the war. He was anxious now to do something, prove to himself that he wasn't getting old – and that he was a good Nazi.

"Would you like another drink, Christian?"

*

Levin first heard drunken laughter on the stairs. The heavy wooden door creaked open. Jakob was curious and petrified as to why this pale-faced man was walking towards him with an ashtray in his hand. Yet still he stood motionless in the corner of the cell. Wolfgang, in a move first rehearsed some years ago during a pogrom, grabbed Jakob by his short hair in his left hand, kicked the backs of his legs so that his feeble victim knelt before him, and poured the contents of the ashtray down his throat. Jakob writhed and such adrenaline was unleashed in his body that he found the strength to release himself from his captor's grasp, flailing his arm up wildly to part Wolfgang's hand from his hair. Jakob fell to the floor and spluttered for dear life. Wolfgang turned to Christian, who was standing by the doorway of the cell, and cackled. Christian expressed a gleeful half-snigger but could not imitate the maniacal, high-pitched laughter which animated his friend.

"Not hungry, Uncle?"

Life is a bully who kicks sand in your face. Is it little wonder that so many people go around with their eyes closed? It is a necessary evil for something, but what? The only way to win is to not take part. Life is a mouthful of ash; that is not to say that there are no honeys to take the taste away, but it is a mouthful of ash. If he died, he died. Jakob was resigned to his fate. This thuggish old man was here to execute him; it was just a matter of how much he would put sadistic pleasure before business. At the end, in the camp, he had observed similar resignation, even relief, on the faces of the men as the guards pressed their pistol barrels into the back of their necks.

"I would have thought, Christian, that he would have tried to look pitiful, to beg or play on our sympathy. Or play dead. But yet there is still some life in this mutt. If you kneel before me Uncle, I will pardon your insolence," Wolfgang playfully issued, his rasping voice rough with a lifetime of cigarettes and bitterness.

Christian, like Wolfgang, had intoxicated play in his eyes but he also felt something else, a discomfort. Yet, trying to stop Wolfgang when he was in a mood like this was even further from his thoughts. He didn't imagine that his friend would go this far when he had suggested (or had Wolfgang suggested it?) that they have some fun with the imprisoned Jew; and besides, hadn't Christian dreamed of this and often desired to transgress? Did not this haughty Jew deserve to be taken down a peg or two?

Jakob remained on his feet, his eyes glinting with shades of dark humour and defiance. Better to die on one's feet than live on one's knees. He would not kneel before this ugly, depraved Nazi.

Death would not define his life.

Wolfgang had planned to force the Jew on his knees to satisfy his desire of kicking the animal across the face. Yet the Jew remained on his feet. Wolfgang took two quick steps, lifted his right leg and brought his heel down upon Jakob's left knee. Something snapped in the back of his leg and the pain throbbed even before Jakob fell to the floor; he gasped for air but his mouth and throat felt like they were peppered with rust. Tears finally seeped from stone; Jakob cowered, crawled, away from his tormentor and, holding his left leg, rocked from side to side.

Wolfgang, drool spilling from his mouth as he spoke, triumphantly stood over his winged prey. The words were just a noise to Jakob; his hands now covering his head, curled up in a protective ball, the captive pressed his eyes shut and prayed for his salvation – his end. Let them put him down like an animal, for man is but an animal – unique as a species only in terms of his capacity for self-delusion and viciousness.

"You are weak, Jew. You are not me. You may think me cruel, but we are saving this world – from you. Only the strongest must survive because only the strongest will survive. Ten of you are not worth one German. I look in the mirror and see strength, health and dignity. What do you see when you look in the mirror, you Christ-murdering vermin?"

Wolfgang interpreted the Jew's silence as being a form of defiance. All along he had intended to murder the Jew in cold blood – but now he would do so in blood-lust, too. Christian could be coerced after the deed. He would win his freedom and besides, if he hated his prisoner as much as he harped on about him, the punishment would be its own reward. Wolfgang would back Christian up in his explanation that the Jew was trying to escape. He removed a small black pistol from his coat pocket. Christian's eyes widened, sucking in the dream-like scene; normality had spiralled out of control; his will now bowed down to that which he was impotent to prevent.

"There is no evil that I have not yet considered."

The sound was like that of a door slamming.

CHAPTER ELEVEN

The door slammed open. Wolfgang and Christian turned around and initially stared at the Wehrmacht officer in shock more than fear. Robert stood entranced for a couple of seconds, his heart bleeding for the waif-like creature shielding himself on the floor. Robert had still not fully recovered from his episodic afternoon – he was like a mind waiting for his body to catch up with him. Disbelief and revelation still infused his heart. To save face – and Jakob – Robert would suddenly have to play the villain, or hero. He fixed his glance at the balding, beak-nosed man who stood over the Jew; the officer wore confidence and a slice of disdain in his expression.

"Put the gun down."

"Do you know who I am?" Wolfgang responded, attempting to echo the authority and calm in the captain's tone.

"A trespasser. Now put the gun down."

Wolfgang lowered his Mauser and put it away. Christian sidestepped into a crevice of the cell. The burly soldier was ashamed, anticipant and now sober.

"Don't dare fill pity for this Jew. Anyone filled with pity is pitiful," Wolfgang sententiously uttered.

"He is working for the state. He is an essential worker. How are you essential to the world?"

Wolfgang gritted his teeth and forced a smile. To extricate himself from this trouble, free from punishment and with his pride intact, Wolfgang would have to call the officer's bluff. He would hint that he was part of the SS, or rather Gestapo. It had worked before with people, acting as though he might be affiliated with the Secret Police. They were a law unto themselves and rightly did not need to explain themselves. Many a time had Wolfgang, his hands laced behind his head upon his pillow, day-dreamed that he was part of their auspicious ranks.

"I would be wary of your tone Captain, you never know who you might be talking to. I have friends."

"You are an amusing fellow, I don't doubt that you have friends."

"I mean I have friends in high places."

"Don't we all know someone in the Luftwaffe? Forgive me also if I judge you by the company you keep," Robert wryly replied, acknowledging Christian in the corner.

Wolfgang felt a film of perspiration form upon his forehead. His face flared up like a petrol fire as the more he tried to puff himself up the more deflated he felt. His ego shrivelled as if it was a slug, with the imposing officer acting as the salt.

"You have no idea just who I am, do you Captain?" The waxen-faced old Nazi shook his head and gently smiled as if to be amused by the Captain's mistaken impression of him compared to the reality.

"You are a coward and a half-wit."

It was as if someone had slapped a glove around the sadist's cheek. His features dropped and the colour drained from his face to reveal his true, demoralised, state of being. Wolfgang felt he had no choice however but to keep up the pretence, even if he was clutching at straws to intimidate his antagonist.

"I may be a few things Captain, but, as sure as night follows day, I can assure you that I am no coward. I am an original Party member and a veteran of the Great War," Wolfgang, chest out, proudly pronounced in a tone which nevertheless betrayed the pinch he was suffering.

"Methinks the lady dost protest too much."

Robert's tone changed to that of being playful; his antagonist was now a source of amusement to him. That this officer didn't even wish to know his name was insult enough to Wolfgang.

"But I am nothing if not fair, my insidious fellow. I will grant you the opportunity to prove me wrong. You may attack me, but I warn you that unlike that poor creature over there, I will hit back," Robert issued.

His blood frothing, Wolfgang was more than tempted to call the arrogant Captain's bluff. And he who hits first, hits hardest; it was the right thing to do. But Wolfgang's internalised rage didn't quite overwhelm his fear and prudence. Albeit his eyes were daggers, Wolfgang merely politely smiled at the captain. Robert smirked back, indeed he was far from putting on an act now, he genuinely wanted to play the villain or hero and teach the fascist a lesson by goading him into a fight. But the bully was a coward.

Wolfgang bared his teeth not.

"Well, my whole-hearted half-wit, I believe you have taken up enough of my time. You may take your leave now. Should you set foot in my house again you will receive a less than friendly welcome."

Robert stood his ground so that the derided Wolfgang had to awkwardly move around him to get out of the door. The mute Christian was also keen to make his exit, but he was sternly called back by his commanding officer.

"You too need never set foot in this house again, Christian. I will send you the necessary papers and you are to sign up for the front."

"But I didn't do anything," his voice quivering like his heart at the officer's decision, knowing and regretting how his whole life had been turned upside down in the space of thirty ill-judged minutes.

"That you didn't do anything is the reason why you should feel ashamed of yourself."

Winded by the news, Christian Boar nevertheless broke into a trot to catch up to his seething and demoralised friend. Occupied with their own thoughts and plans they exchanged little conversation on their way back to Wolfgang's cramped, damp apartment.

Robert was left alone with his still whimpering and half oblivious prisoner. The captain was wary of picking Jakob up at first for fear of breaking the enfeebled, brittle figure, but Robert knew that he had to help the man; compassion and purpose felt natural and authoritative, as if the veil had been lifted from his eyes. Something had broken inside of the troubled soul, but at the same time something had also slotted into place.

CHAPTER TWELVE

The thick, sweet odour of disinfectant and ammonia ousted out the aroma of the watery broth they were distributing in the hospital canteen. Exhausted doctors and nurses, their coats tinged with various beige and crimson stains, looked barely healthier than some of the distressed and atrophied casualties. A metallic clang, as a meal tray crashed to the floor, arrested the attention of most of the staff and patients alike. Only a young nurse and doctor sitting in the corner together carried on with their conversation and supper as if nothing had happened, being all too used to the event.

In her coarse grey uniform and wimple, one could have mistaken the young nurse, Charlotte Friedrich, for a novice. One could sometimes be at pains to guess her age. Her green marble eyes, when one caught her off guard in private, were as sorrowful and wise as a mother's. Only when she smiled (her genuine smile, not the one she habitually wore to soothe or cheer up her patients) did Charlotte betray her virginal twenty-one years. But Charlotte was no mere adolescent girl. Over the past eighteen months Charlotte had blossomed into a woman. Despite or because of the rigours of her duties and hours, she had shed the teenage puppy fat from her face; her features and figure were becoming increasingly taut and elegant. A small scar below and to the right of her bottom lip was the only blemish on a fair, ivory complexion.

Charlotte's mother, Evelina, had died shortly after her being born but one could easily contest that the child's development, both intellectually and emotionally, did not suffer from her father's sole parentage. From an early age Charlotte was a bright and inquisitive child, though a stubborn and melancholy streak were also ingrained in her make up. Never really concerned with toys or frivolity, Charlotte found contentment and a release in the involving worlds of the books that she read. She devoured the European canon as if it were going out of fashion, and also immersed herself in English literature. Although far from shy or unsociable, Charlotte, even and especially in her teens, preferred the company of her father and the elder members of her family, rather than her peers. Intelligent and proud at an early age, Charlotte often looked down on the immature amusements and role-playing of her would-be girlfriends. So too she looked down upon, as well as saw through, the scores of moronic, homogenized German boys who would have courted her should she have given them the opportunity. And who could stand comparison with the Danish Princes, Werthers, D'artangans and other chivalrous heroes who populated Charlotte's world? The only boy who Charlotte did have any time or affection for in her adolescence was Joshua, a Jewish boy who wanted to be a doctor. But his family had got him out of the country before the war; and didn't Charlotte really own an attachment to Joshua out of pity and sympathy?

Charlotte's freedom from the prejudices of other youths her age was mainly due to her liberal, journalist father's decision to educate his daughter as much from home as in a state school. For the most part, Karl Friedrich freely allowed his daughter to sit in on his evening discussions with his friends concerning the injustices that the state and that 'odious, Austrian male Circe' were perpetrating. Even when it grew late and Charlotte was sent to bed she would often creep back down the stairs again, carefully avoiding the creaking step, and carry on being absorbed by the conversation, being taken back sometimes by her father's blazing indignation and colourful language.

Not long after the outbreak of the war Karl Friedrich left his daughter in the care of Charlotte's favourite uncle, a teddy bear of a man called Hermann who doted upon his niece. Shortly afterwards he disappeared during the act of helping some Jews get out of the country. Charlotte had not heard from her father since, although friends and family tried to assure her that he had probably not got in contact with her for fear of compromising himself – and more importantly endangering Charlotte. Nevertheless, the girl's melancholy streak had deepened as a result of her father's fate. In a way, despite the gory and disheartening scenes she daily witnessed, Charlotte's vocation as a nurse saved her from maudlin reflections and self-absorbed dejection. Work kept her purposeful *("Employment is nature's physician, essential to human happiness." Galen)*. Possessing a serious and compassionate nature, Charlotte hesitated not in her decision to become a nurse, particularly when she realised how desperate the need was in the town's still over-worked and under-staffed hospital. Despite having second thoughts when initially plunged in at the deep end, when the arduous daily grind did not live up to her idealised picture of the profession, Charlotte focused herself even more and her doubts and deficiencies were bested. Indeed, working day-to-day in the hospital had strengthened rather than punctured her belief in the need for acts of goodness in this world – and that just because something is a losing battle, that doesn't mean that one shouldn't fight it. But the nurse had long concluded that her country's war machine wasn't worth the blood-shed to maintain and lubricate it. "If not for the awful reality of the thing, I would laugh at the irony that they say that this war is being fought in the name of peace," her father had once said. But even without the speeches and realised prophesies of Karl Friedrich, his sensible daughter would have grown to resent the fraudulence and cruelties of the state she was living under; she suffered in not only being able to diagnose the maladies, but equally Charlotte felt despair at being unable to administer the remedy. Kill or cure had now become just kill for Charlotte. Her prayer for peace was linked to that of praying for defeat. Yet the bold young woman wisely kept such thoughts and sentiments to herself.

Charlotte Friedrich's companion at supper on this day, as he was on many occasions, was Stefan Numan, a twenty-five year old doctor. The smell of coffee upon his breath was one of the few odours pungent enough to be noticed above the disinfectant.

The Finnish doctor's eyes were red from a lack of sleep and from his constant rubbing of them to stay awake; his straight, long, almost white-blonde hair was lank and his face seemed to be as perpetually clammy as his hands. Stefan told himself that he had become so attracted to Charlotte over the past year because she had matured and he admired her professionalism as a nurse, but really the repressed doctor had grown physically attracted to the now nubile, pretty assistant. Charlotte could make his day with just a smile – and aroused and animated his dreams at night. Yet the diffident doctor rightly sensed that Charlotte did not feel the same about him as he did about her, and so refrained from crossing their professional and platonic relationship boundary – hopeful as he was that things could change after the war. She was worth the wait, he soberly concluded. Stefan noticed how other doctors and soldiers had tried to court the nurse and, as a result, Charlotte had cooled her friendships with the would-be suitors.

An intrusive shadow loomed over the couple's table to interrupt their conversation. Hans Riedle, the bureaucratic senior administrator of the hospital, stood before them.

"Ah, Charlotte, here you are. I couldn't find you on the ward. I have an urgent job for you. Could you please go over to this address? A good friend of mine, and the hospital's I might add, needs some medical assistance for someone in his household."

Charlotte read the piece of paper she was handed and raised her eyebrow. Stefan, not taking his surveying eyes off the object of his affection all the while, greedily wanted to know what had stimulated this strange response in that face which he thought he had numbered all the expressions of. The good doctor's heart skipped a beat, itching out of curiosity for a second, but then flared up upon Charlotte's revelation.

"Robert Fischer?"

"What, Captain Robert Fischer?" Stefan ejaculated – his eyes stapled wide open.

"Yes."

"I wouldn't mind it sir if you let me go instead," Stefan purposefully inserted, his gallantry a little too pronounced.

"No, I need you here. There will be a batch of fresh casualties arriving from the Front soon."

"Then we will need every available member of staff here, including Charlotte."

"This is not a matter for debate, doctor. I'm sure Charlotte will be perfectly fine, she is an experienced nurse and a big girl now."

"With respect sir, it is not Charlotte who I am worried about. You yourself know his reputation. For God's sake you yourself told me about the rumour."

"Which rumour?" Charlotte asked, more intrigued than a feared – the latter being the desired effect that her protective colleague wished to instil in the young woman.

"Stefan, don't," Hans warned, pursing his thin lips and trying to look stern.

"Apparently, some years ago, the Captain had an affair with a doctor's wife. When the husband, a former cavalry officer, found out he challenged the rake to an old fashioned duel. When it came to the day however the doctor graciously fired up into the air. In reply to this though Fischer took aim and shot him in the head, murdering him. When his second demanded why he had done such a thing Fischer, in a tone as cold as ice, apparently answered that by shooting him in the head he had spared the widow the expense of an open coffin. There is also the talk that Fischer is keeping a Jew prisoner in his house who is doing work for the state."

"Might I also remind you doctor of the fact, not rumour, that Captain Fischer is one of the most generous patrons of this hospital."

Robert was indeed one of the most generous patrons of the hospital. His accountant made sure Robert donated enough monies to charity in order to achieve tax exemptions on the rest of his estate. Not only was Hans Riedle grateful to the wealthy philanthropist for his donations to the hospital but, out of gratitude for doing him this favour of letting him have one of his nurses, the influential captain might also introduce him to his social circle at the club that both men were members of.

"I appreciate your worrying about me Stefan, but I'll be fine," Charlotte said, kindly smiling at her colleague but consoling him little. "Whether the story is true or not I doubt if the captain will call me out for a duel. As long as you can spare me sir, I'll go."

"Thank you, Charlotte. I dare say you will find Robert to be a gentleman."

After the nurse got up from the table to fetch the requisite first aid kit that she believed she might need for the house call, Stefan sulkily remarked to his self-serving superior, "Aye, didn't someone once say that the prince of darkness is a gentleman?"

CHAPTER THIRTEEN

An hour or so later Charlotte was standing before and gazing up at the gothic influenced nineteenth century house. The young nurse blew air out of the side of her mouth to try and cool her flustered, rain freckled face. She rallied one more time, told herself not to be intimidated by the captain, and forcefully rang the bell. A kind of national socialist devoted Peggoty answered the door, her rosy cheeks were so round as to protrude out from her face as much as her nose. Her apron was awash with more stains than a coroner's. Calling the nurse 'dearie' Frau Huber bustled the girl into the house. Charlotte darted glances all around her at the tastefully decorated residence – the beautiful pastoral art and imported English furniture – as the sanguine maid took the nurse up to her master's bedroom. As elegant and opulent as the furnishings of the house were though, Charlotte felt an absence of homeliness, or warmth, towards the grand old property.

Only when the maid shut the door on her way out, after introducing Charlotte, did Robert fully wake from his reverie. He had been tending to the resting Jakob (if tending to Jakob meant glaring at him as if he were a corpse) with his back towards the door. For a few moments he still vacantly stared at the nurse, but then he quickly came to his senses and greeted the young woman.

"Thank you for coming, Miss…?"

"Charlotte Friedrich, Captain," Charlotte replied, the very soul of formality.

Robert was surprised by the age of the nurse and for a second doubted her abilities and experience, but yet more than that he was just relieved that the social-climbing hospital administrator had finally sent him someone.

Even in her heavy, unflattering uniform Robert thought that the girl possessed an enviable figure. One could even divine her shapely calves and pretty ankles beneath her thick black stockings. Her mouth and blonde, arching eyebrows were expressive; her clean, silvery voice and poise betrayed a stifling, bourgeois background. Her eyelashes were naturally curled and even coquettish. She was no great beauty, Robert considered, but she was naturally, uncommonly pretty.

She has something about her.

During this brief pause in which the Captain took in this round faced, snub nosed and soft-chinned nurse, Charlotte's eyes flitted around the room, in order to both survey her surroundings and not return the captain's awkward glance. Yet she couldn't help but survey the infamous officer as well. She had to admit that Herr Fischer was as handsome as she had heard – but still not to her taste. That beauty is not conducive to virtue, Charlotte had long realised. Monsters come in all different shapes and sizes. But he was handsome, if a little scornful looking. Charlotte received the impression that the captain was preoccupied, as though he was either remembering or trying to memorize something when she had come in and disturbed him. Yet Charlotte's coy, brief contemplation of the gossiped about officer was curtailed as she felt a couple of strands of hair drop down her face, which she tucked back into her starched wimple.

Maria and her elitist set would have deemed her plain but, if she made the effort, perhaps this young nurse could have been demure enough to provoke a comment from Maria borne from envy rather than general, inherent, bitchiness, the officer would speculate. There is no word in German for adorable, but nevertheless as she smoothed her sunshine-coloured hair back into place and shyly avoided the officer's intimidating aspect, Charlotte might have impressed upon Robert how veritably adorable she was; her modesty made her all the more attractive (but the officer also sardonically judged that the nurse had a lot to be modest about).

Charlotte motioned her head around the officer to prompt him into concerning themselves with the patient. She reproached herself for her lack of professionalism at not attending to the patient immediately.

"I am sorry, Miss Friedrich, for calling you out at so late an hour but my friend – "

"If he is your friend, Captain, I do not envy your enemies," Charlotte coldly interjected. By now the near indignant nurse had scurried around the captain and was at the prisoner's bedside. Jakob looked like a cadaverous figure from Hogarth; his cheeks were hollow, his black eyes were in disproportion to his face like an owl's. Although seemingly at death's door Jakob was semi-conscious – and thankfully in a better condition than he appeared. Only Charlotte's immediate and maternal pity for the prisoner tempered her impulse to condemn his loathsome jailer. Right now he was just in the way and preventing her from doing her job properly.

"I feel you should just leave now Captain, before I say something that might do neither of us much credit."

Charlotte's tone was matronly and even schoolmarmish. It seemed peculiar, almost comical – this adolescent nurse adopting a high moral tone and lecturing Robert Fischer. But her heart was emboldened by contempt and pity. She uttered a few more words under her breath which Robert did not catch, but they sounded equally indignant. Not since university had someone dared to castigate and at the same time patronise him. He had repaid his lecturer then by slashing his tyres immediately after his righteous, hypocritical speech, but here Robert absorbed the judgement. He was thankful that the nurse was rude and dismissive towards him - enough to keep her back to him whilst damning the object of her righteous scorn; the guilty captain didn't feel worthy enough to look anyone in the eye at this point. Robert bit his lip and wondered if he should ask the nurse if she needed anything. He imagined though that should he say another word the nurse might break out into hysterics or lash out and claw at his eyes; he imagined it because maybe he desired it; he deserved it.

"If you need anything, Miss Friedrich – please let me know."

"I think you have done enough Captain, don't you? I only need you to leave us alone."

The officer moved from biting his lip to theoretically biting his tongue. A man can only accept so much humility – and Robert was in virgin territory. How dare this girl reproach him? As perceptive and genuine as her thoughts may have been concerning what had happened to Jakob, they were still borne from sensibility and not sense. What proof had she to blindly make him responsible and guilty? Did she know who she was talking to? – Robert would argue, internally. But nevertheless the officer retreated out of the room, somewhat sheepishly. Only pangs of hunger motivated him not to take himself to bed in one of his spare rooms. The officer politely asked one of his maids to make him something to eat and to bring it to him in his study. He also instructed her to look in on the nurse and prisoner and ask them if they wanted anything. Before entering his study Robert descended into the basement and retrieved Jakob's translations. He wondered if the Ministry of Propaganda would be suspicious or curious if the stream of work he had been sending them dried up whilst Levin recovered? But the captain suddenly formulated an idea to take care of that particular potential problem.

CHAPTER FOURTEEN

After a simple, satisfying meal of steamed haddock and boiled potatoes, Robert collected his thoughts and decided to proceed with his plan. He didn't really know why he was doing it. Was some lowly civil servant really going to be fastidious enough as to investigate why the project to translate some unexceptional poetry had slowed to a halt? But Robert was not going to take the chance. The German state had become both a hydra-headed and a leviathan over the past decade. Jakob had to continue to be thought of as essential, even if the officer had to prove it by false means. The nurse was tending to his injuries but it was Robert's responsibility to keep Levin alive. Robert also found the idea of duping the ministry quite amusing by sending them some of his own poetry which he had composed in his youth – when poetry and love mean something to a man. He carefully took the fading manuscript out of the brown envelope which he kept in the only locked draw of his study. It had been about five years now since he last read these fragments composed so fondly and vainly. Nostalgia provoked a philosophical smile from the captain and softened his worried features. Yes, he could still feel a wedge of embarrassment for the Romeo and Onegin who had so soulfully composed these pieces, but he was sufficiently distanced from that bad poet and idealist to laugh as much at him as with him. And were some of the fragments not without glimpses of wit and technical merit? Robert brushed the film of dust off the top sheet, surprised that in a sealed envelope in a locked draw there could be such a thing. Is nothing sacred to decay? Writing under the pseudonym of one Richard Brooking, Fischer began to copy out some of his poetry, the following piece being the chief work he completed that evening.

An Abridged Poem.

The memory of you pours again now
Like cavalry down the Avalon vale
To the grunt of my heart.
Why is my training for this all so poor
When thou'rt as regular as morning? Your
Sword cleaves the air apart.

So an infantry square I marshal, form,
In respect of this blood-curdling storm.
Time tempers not the scar.
I know full well I'm no match for vict'ry;
But to keep my colour, taste dignity.
I'll break not ------.

Captained by Pride, a Duty to that Pride
And Revenge I stand alone, side by side.
Cavalries break not squares.
But still you tear down the hill like a flood
Re-writing the book of love in my blood.
Oh brothers say your prayers.

Unleashed like a fury I smell her now.
Oh to forget that smile, kiss; fair is foul.
My memory's too good.
My memory's too good to loss allow.
To forget thy my soul's flogging and how
You'd save me if you could.

Pride was shamed and Duty to Pride fell first.
Revenge turned on himself; the square was cursed
By her still, thrusting eye.
Her oeilliards brought chaos to the ranks.
I noticed to Lucifer she gave thanks
Ere, to myself, I cried.

Lust was first to sever from the square's womb;
Hope and forgiveness soon livened the tomb,
Hope the vilest sinner.
The rest is history for she got in
And carved down my comp'ny easy as sin.
Ni'lism the winner.

Robert put his pen down and read over this last line with wry grief upon his face. He had been a widower in all but name. The past is never completely in the past. But he was content with his work - for once his words would speak as loudly as action. But, physically and emotionally drained, Robert bowed to the inevitable. Resting his heavy head on his folded arms on the desk he drifted off into a palliative slumber - too exhausted to even dream.

CHAPTER FIFTEEN

Jakob was now conscious, if still a little docile and delirious. The time during which the proficient but tender nurse had treated, bathed and clothed him had passed like a phase of hypnogogic sleep. She had also spoon-fed him with some kind of soup or stew. Charlotte was pleased to observe that the patient possessed an appetite. After feeding him, the prisoner drifted back off to sleep. Whilst before Levin looked dead to the world, now he seemed at peace with it. It was three o'clock in the morning, the moonless evening engulfed the sight of the buildings across the street and even muffled out the shine of the chrome bumpers on the cars below. The air was peppered with rain and when the wind changed direction it sounded upon the bedroom window pane like a distant tinny drum marching off into a faraway battle. Charlotte looked at her watch again but decided that she wouldn't leave until her patient fully woke up again and she could assess his condition. From working evenings in the hospital the nurse had grown used to long hours so this arduous night could've hardly been described as such. She took off her wimple and relaxed in the chair. Her hair was the colour of candlelight, full-bodied and shoulder blade length. Yet, as beautiful as her body of hair was, "the picture is still worth more than the frame" - as her uncle often fondly told her.

Jakob stirred and woke up, aware of the fact that it was no longer a dream. The withered Jew gazed up at the fair nurse and tried to smile. It was here that Charlotte realised that she was acquainted with her patient.

"Mr Levin?"

"Charlotte Friedrich?" Jakob croaked.

Smiles were increasingly beamed and reciprocated, after their initial sense of disbelief subsided. Jakob had been Charlotte's private tutor in her early teens. A friend of her father's, Jakob had been hired a few months after he was released from his position at the university. She remembered him as having, like her father, a particularly dry sense of humour, if indeed Mr Levin had a sense of humour in the conventional understanding of the term. She recalled how the scholar could always divine whether Charlotte was being truly honest or not. She remembered how his thick black eyebrow was permanently, funnily arched when he read the newspaper, yet he would rarely comment on an article. Her father would often get frustrated with Mr Levin for him not being angry or reacting enough to things. As a teacher Charlotte remembered how Mr Levin always answered her questions, which were many and sometimes naïve the nurse would now have to admit, with a question himself – 'Every answer should provoke another question,' she remembered him saying. But Mr Levin was an excellent tutor who Charlotte recalled with fondness if for no other reason than he introduced her to Henry James and Christina Rossetti.

"Despite the circumstances, it's nice to see you again Charlotte."

Never one for expressions of affection, Levin nevertheless felt the sudden desire, which was gratified, to squeeze Charlotte's hand.

"Thank you Charlotte," Jakob, almost pathetically, remarked.

"That you are feeling better is thanks enough, Mr Levin."

The young woman sounded like a schoolgirl again as she called him 'Mr Levin', but that was who he was to Charlotte; he was 'Mr Levin', one of her favourite teachers.

"I think that you are allowed to call me Jakob now Charlotte."

Jakob's face cracked into a smile.

"Tell me, how is your father?"

Only now, when he was engaging in it, did Jakob realise how much he had missed simple, polite conversation in receptive company. He gazed at Charlotte with almost paternal pride to see how genuinely pretty she had become. Her eyes lost their lustre however as he asked this question. Her chin sunk into her chest and Charlotte began to fidget with the wimple that rested on her lap.

"Papa has been missing for years. He disappeared whilst trying to help some people get out of the country. I am now living with my uncle."

Jakob didn't witness the sorrow and awkwardness in Charlotte's face. Before the nurse even completed her sentence Jakob, troubled, turned his head back up to the ceiling. Their pasts haunted them both. The momentary silence which occurred between them would have been uncomfortable if one of them had noticed it but both figures were bound up like a knot with themselves. But Jakob wasn't going to be dragged down by the weight of History, or rather he would not let the girl be dragged down by its unpleasant memories.

"It's nice to see that you have remained fair."

The softly spoken Jew was not being inconsiderate or cowardly in changing the subject so dramatically; his intention, which Charlotte appreciated, was to be comforting, distracting. She ran her hand through her hair again, absorbing the warm, massaging sensation.

"I have no idea how I've stayed fair. What with my hours at the hospital I rarely see the light of day. It is both a civilian and military hospital. The casualties from the Front seem to be growing in number every week. If you do not mind me asking, why are you here, being detained in this house?"

"I am still considered to be an essential worker. I have been commissioned, so to speak, to translate English poetry into German. There are worse fates," Jakob issued, offering a sprained smile.

"If you are an essential worker then the captain should take better care of you. To think that at the hospital there are some people who have nothing but praise for him – principally because he seems to be as rich as sin. I just hope that the Russian army have as much respect for him as I do," Charlotte replied, her eyes darkly ablaze.

Jakob was briefly preoccupied in thought. At the same time as trying to bury such nightmarish visions and fears that are best left buried, he tried to revive the memories he had of the officer and the episode. As if to himself more than Charlotte, Jakob exclaimed, as if he were a teacher again,

"I believe that he saved my life. Do not be too quick to judge the captain, Charlotte. No one can know the full story of a man, see the whole picture. We are always somewhat in the dark. Do not solely judge a man's present and future by what he has done in the past."

*

Robert attempted to knock on the door at such an audible level so as to warn the nurse that he was entering, but quiet enough so as to not disturb Jakob should he be sleeping. To his surprise when he entered, Robert discovered the pair both awake and animated, talking like old school friends. And, like old school friends, they became conspicuously silent when a stranger came into their midst.

"Miss Friedrich," Robert said, acknowledging the wet-fish looking nurse with a slight nod of his head. However, he quickly shifted his attention to the patient, unintentionally being rude.

"Are you feeling better, Jakob?"

Robert made sure that his tone was neither patronising nor dispassionate. Jakob accepted the good-natured concern for good-natured concern, albeit he was still suspicious of this change of heart in the egotistical officer.

"I am feeling much better Captain, thank you. I believe I must also thank you for – "

"You have nothing to thank me for Jakob. Rather, I am sorry."

For two people who were strangers to displaying gratitude and contrition, a brief telemetry was achieved between the guilt of one and attempted absolution of the other. It was all written in their expressions; words killeth. Charlotte was pricked to see the captain appear so vulnerable. Could she be wrong about him? If she was wrong then nobody else was right. But still she didn't trust the selfish officer and simmered with resentment for him, or rather his uniform. Jakob finally broke the eloquent silence.

"I will get back to my work as soon as possible, Captain."

"There's no rush, I have taken care of it. Just rest and concentrate on regaining your strength Jakob – and ceasing in calling me captain."

"I am surprised to find myself agreeing with the captain, Jakob. You should just focus on recovering. Your knee will take some time to fully heal, as will your general constitution."

Robert smiled to himself, amused by the nurse's prejudices towards him – prejudices he could play on.

"I would not dare try and alter your opinion of me, but may I surprise you again by inviting you to stay the night, Miss Friedrich? It is late. It is also the least I can do. I must insist that you sleep in one of the guest bedrooms, however. As much as you believe that you know me, I warrant I do not know you well enough for any other sleeping arrangement."

"I have a sense of humour Captain, but I find you more sarcastic than amusing."

"Really, Miss Friedrich? I find myself sarcastic and amusing in equal measure but, unlike you, I do not have much of a sense of humour."

Jakob rightly sensed that the nail upon Charlotte's Catherine Wheel of a temper was coming loose. He duly eased himself between the skirmishing couple.

"If for no other reason, would you stay for me, Charlotte? I cannot tell you how much I have enjoyed your company. I used to tutor Charlotte, Captain."

"Really?"

"You are surprised that a woman might be highly educated, Captain?"

"No. Unfortunately very little surprises me, Miss Friedrich."

"Warfare is not the sole point of our existence. You may be shocked to hear that with a little learning we may raise ourselves above our barbarous inheritance."

"A little learning is a dangerous thing,

Drink deep or taste not the Pierian spring."

Should Charlotte not have been so incensed and nettled by the arrogant captain and his condescending tone, then she might have admired the officer's knowledge of poetry and the ease with which he slipped into speaking English. Jakob Levin however couldn't help but duly note the Captain's depth of learning and ironist's sensibility.

"Even the devil can quote Shakespeare," Charlotte answered,

proud of the wit and swiftness of her reply. Her polished features soon changed however after Robert's final parry and thrust, to which the young woman found no answer. Albeit Robert consciously did not give her an opportunity to reply.

"Actually the couplet is from Pope, though your guess was not an altogether incompetent one, Miss Friedrich. If you are but half as tired as I am Jakob, then I should take my leave of you now. I would certainly prefer a good night's sleep to my company. Should you wish Miss Friedrich, I will show you to a guest bedroom. I will talk to you again tomorrow, if that is okay with you, Jakob?"

"Yes, that will be fine. Thank you again."

A thought combed through Jakob's head, that this polite act could be just that, an act; a sick, ultimately sadistic joke. Is imprisonment not rendered crueller for tasting freedom? Is misery not compounded when one has fallen from joy? While this cold, plausible chain of thought ploughed on in Levin's mind he barely noticed Charlotte wishing him goodnight, and tenderly kissing him upon the forehead, before departing with Captain Fischer. Finally, thankfully, maternal sleep kissed the brittle academic's eyelids.

CHAPTER SIXTEEN

Charlotte walked a couple of paces behind the officer as he led her down a narrow candlelit passage. It was so dimly lit that the nurse could've surrendered to the childish impulse she felt – to screw her face up and poke her tongue out at her rude host, free from detection in the shadows. But Charlotte was too busy dissecting and condemning the captain to expend her energies on such pettiness. He was an arrogant snob; since leaving the bedroom the officer hadn't spoken a word to the nurse. He hadn't even deigned to look at her. Did he think Charlotte unworthy of his conversation? Did she serve the purpose as a source of amusement and nothing else? He was little more than a spoilt child – no doubt his treatment of Charlotte was some kind of perverse revenge for the way she had spoken to him when they first met. He was antagonistic towards her because she saw him for what he was; the mystery (vanity) which you had to unlock was that the captain wished to appear enigmatic. No doubt he thought his aloofness made him more attractive; if one appears dark enough one may fool a person into believing that there is depth where shallowness resides. If only he was as unattractive as his black heart, then his wit would be taken for facetiousness and his morals would rightly be judged as immoral. He would then be ostracised from the high society which lauded him. Goodness should no more be mistaken for Beauty as it should be synonymous with Knowledge, the nurse posited. Charlotte was glad that the elitist officer thought her unworthy of conversation; the more divorced she was from this Narcissus, the better.

Robert could feel the spirited nurse simmer as she walked behind him; possessing the power to bring her to the boil at an ill (well) chosen word was satisfaction enough for him not to overcook her. He hoped that her God could forgive her for all the names she was probably now calling him behind his back. The priggish girl was no doubt deeming him a child and obnoxious at this point; if there was vinegar in the honey she might also be concluding how vain he was, that he thought himself to be some kind of superior or Byronic figure. Just for her folly though he would here briefly be the choreographer of the nurse's body, as well as the author of her thoughts. Believing the wilful girl to be preoccupied with her silent tirade against him Robert abruptly stopped dead still, and allowed Charlotte to bump into him. She kicked his heels and her hands pressed against his back; the nurse quickly recoiled with all the disgust of the repelled tone of her thoughts but nevertheless Charlotte momentarily felt both ridiculous and decentred – the two things which she promised herself she would not feel in his presence anymore.

"I apologise Charlotte, but here is your room."

He called her Charlotte for the first time in a subtle but

detectably sardonic tone. Yet, as vexed as she was, Charlotte took the reins of her excitable horses and returned mock politeness with mock politeness.

"Thank you, Captain," Charlotte replied whilst stabbing out a sour smile. Although Charlotte felt uncomfortable dealing in such an artificial manner, she was more than willing to suffer her behaviour in order to wipe the amused smirk off the glib officer's face.

"I hope the room is to your liking, Miss Friedrich."

"I do not believe I could suffer any more offence this evening, Captain Fischer."

"You underestimate me, Miss Friedrich."

Robert now broke into a grin; his expression was warm and harmless. It was a countenance now filled with understanding and charm rather than smugness, hoping to coax out of Charlotte the conclusion that he was but being playful, rather than serious, in his relations with the girl.

Charlotte was determined not to reciprocate or approve of the Nazi's smarmy and indecent behaviour. So self-satisfied was he that he could smile alone. She would not excuse his sins as easily as his sycophantic and decadent social set, she vowed.

"I neither underestimate nor overestimate you, Captain. In point of fact I think little or nothing of you," Charlotte asserted with relish.

"Please do not think too ill of me Miss Friedrich, I can assure you I do enough of that for the both of us. Indeed I would genuinely like you to think more of me, as I would, too. Now, if you will excuse me, I should retire. Good night," Robert softly and vulnerably replied in a dramatically altered voice. The solemn officer knitted his brow and walked back down the corridor, her cold words still flickering in his ears. He couldn't help but spare a thought for the spirited young nurse that night. She was both intelligent and proud for her age; for all of her modesty she was as outwardly pretty as she was inwardly virtuous and compassionate, a rare commodity in an age where appearances sufficed for merit and reality. He could and he couldn't understand and appreciate her antagonism towards him. Her hair was uncommonly beautiful and for a time, Robert could not get the picture out of his mind of Charlotte tenderly caressing Jakob's cheek and softly kissing him upon the forehead as she wished him 'good night' and he drifted off to sleep. He reproached himself – for only now, when it was perhaps too late, did he desire to make a good impression on the admirable woman.

Initially Charlotte was suspicious of the captain's parting words, believing them to be a sarcastic prologue to another witticism from him. In the aftermath of their exchange however Charlotte became increasingly shocked and intrigued. Certainly the Captain had begun by piquing Charlotte, but yet in that pause, comma, at the close of their conversation, it was as if the officer was possessed by some spirit of sincerity or uneasy confession – and his words were turned into Darcy-like prose. If he was being insincere, then why was he so critical of himself? A genuine melancholy seemed to envelope him. Perhaps the captain was not aloof, but alone.

Charlotte stood in her spartanly furnished room. The bed was a four-poster and her lilac sheets were silk, but other than that the room just contained an old teak wardrobe and matching chest of draws. When she undressed and went to hang her cardboard uniform in the wardrobe she couldn't help but note the single garment contained within it, a sequined turquoise ball gown that Charlotte briefly fancied would have matched her eyes. Yet, although the debutante's lifestyle was once open to her, Charlotte would not now sacrifice her dowdy uniform for an elegant ball gown; she wouldn't be Charlotte Friedrich if she wasn't a nurse and a Protestant she stated to herself, devoutly. But, despite telling herself that she was content with her lot, her face sank into wistfulness. She was sad, not only because Europe was at war and her father was missing. Certain conceits could sustain her no longer, that there was no one good enough for her or that she enjoyed being unattached – free. There was a hole in her life.

Before the mirror which was perched on top of her chest of drawers the nubile young woman, dressed in a simple white cotton petticoat, sat brushing her long, luxuriant hair. Charlotte studied the bust in the oval glass and thought herself pretty. Jakob had said that she was in bloom; he asked her if being in love was responsible. She had blushed and replied no. The only blemish on her features, which proved barely noticeable in the mirror, was the tiny cross-shaped scar between her lip and chin. She found herself passing her tongue over the smooth, soft membrane of skin. And all the while she brushed and sensuously played with her curls, crimping and caressing herself with her hands. A pea of discomfort was felt beneath her mattress in the bed however as Charlotte's thoughts began to be attracted to the captain again – even her feelings of antipathy towards the egotist drew herself to him. Was she unfair in thinking the worst of the officer? How old was he? Why wasn't he married? Just because she had been the victim of his wit and humour it did not mean that he could not be amusing or engaging; so too behind such an acerbic wit there must have also been a perceptive intelligence – as much as it seemed to be going to waste. Charlotte began to view the Captain in an analytical instead of a critical light; she found him intriguing – from a psychological point of view. The private Robert Fischer was a different person to the notorious officer the town speculated upon. Until now she had thought that it was a result of Jakob's delirium that he believed that the Captain had saved his life, after all he wasn't sure, and the captain had admitted that Jakob had no need to thank him. But was there some truth in the story? As much as Charlotte could bestow the odd redeeming feature on the haunting face of her reverie, the conceited captain could not be completely redeemed in her eyes. Not only at heart was he a German officer but Charlotte had already cemented in her mind an opinion of the petty tyrant – and from previous experiences her first impressions and judgements often proved to be qualified and correct. From an early age Charlotte had prided herself on her high standards and as being an excellent judge of character.

CHAPTER SEVENTEEN

Renewed, Robert woke up at about one in the afternoon and ventured straight downstairs towards the kitchen. No sooner did Charlotte enter his thoughts than he encountered the young nurse on the banisters. She was carrying lunch up to her patient and Charlotte couldn't help but bow her head and bashfully smile at the captain. He grinned back knowing how he must've appeared to the nurse; his un-brushed hair betrayed a double crown, his stubble always looked comically much darker than his hair, his shirt was only half tucked into his trousers and his eyes were as black as they were red. Robert yawned and then smiled that smile that had failed so successfully the previous evening.

"I am pleased to see that you are no longer taking me so seriously, Miss Friedrich."

Robert looked as scruffy this morning as he had been regimentally attired last night; he looked half hung over and half drunk, vulnerable yet endearing. This time Charlotte bathed in the captain's corsair grin. For once she would give the man the benefit of the doubt – and the feeling felt peculiar but good. She tried to bite her bottom lip in order not to smile so much herself.

Charlotte didn't wish to display how she was thawing before the officer, nor did she want to give the impression that she was laughing at him instead of with him. The dawn had somehow dissolved the clouds of animosity and the prejudices of the previous night. A new day had brought a new chapter.

"I hope you do not think that because I have given out an apology already in the last twenty-four hours that I give them out as freely as I do Miss Friedrich, but – "

"There is no need to apologise Captain, we bleed on both sides."

"Hamlet?" Robert replied, pleasantly surprised and impressed.

"Yes."

Both characters smiled at each other with warmth and conciliation gleaming in their features, neither of them quite being aware that they were smiling so. Robert yawned again, blinked repeatedly and lazily placed his hand over his mouth. He then fixed his gaze at the softly steaming meal on Charlotte's tray.

"That smells nice."

"Would you like me to make you some?"

"It's kind of you to offer, but no thank you."

"I'm just taking it up to Jakob in his room, Captain. Are you sure you wouldn't like to join us for lunch?"

"I dare say that I should freshen up first."

"Yes, as hungry as Jakob might be I fear you might put him off his food," Charlotte cheekily but cordially replied.

"For you Miss Friedrich, I will change," Robert retorted, charmingly.

The usually impassive Captain again smiled at this perfect

stranger with not a little wonder in his eyes. His features, as well as his being, were relaxed and expressive. For her part Charlotte gazed up at the enigmatic captain and smiled also, or might we even have called it a simper? How had they not enjoyed each other's company and humour before? The pair squeezed by each other on the back stairs. As Robert did so he was struck by how fine and lively the girl's jade coloured eyes were; in contrast to last night when they had appeared grey and blazed coldly, they were now a Mediterranean blue-green awash with verve and femininity. Robert noticed the small unassuming silver cross upon a chain above Charlotte's breast, which rose and fell more dramatically than usual due to her irregularly beating heart.

The normally serious nurse could barely suppress the feline grin on her face as she entered Jakob's room. Her patient was awake but Charlotte was a little disarmed by how morbid he appeared. An emasculated Levin noticed not her entrance, his attention being focused, like an accountant doing his books. Levin was thinking about Sara. Quite evidently he could live without her – and he could never concede that his 'happiness' had depended upon her – but as Levin mused upon his absent wife all her appealing and virtuous features fizzed their way up like champagne bubbles into Jakob's consciousness: her patience, kindness, ability to engender trust and warmth. Her goodness hurt. Jakob remembered how Sara would always wake before him, despite his early starts, and have his breakfast ready and shirts freshly pressed. He felt the softness of the pillows beneath his head and recalled how, when they were first married, Sara would rest her downy raven tresses on his chest, her slender limbs entwined in his. But that was but a honeymoon period when the young teacher was married to his wife, rather than to his work. Their marriage had not so much been arranged as encouraged by their well-matched families. At the time he was no more averse to getting married as to not getting married – and the shy young man was far from dissatisfied with the wife contingent forces had picked out for him (she had an enviable figure, was neither unintelligent nor demanding – and wasn't typically Jewish looking which was also aesthetically pleasing for Jakob). Indeed one could've argued that it was Jakob and not Sara who had done better out of the match, or *the transaction* as he sometimes labelled the whole thing in private. Sara was certainly a better wife than Jakob was a husband. But had she understood that whenever he had uttered "I don't care" in one of his moods and shrugged his shoulders to such questions involving neighbourhood gossip or meal choices, that it was the subject, not Sara, that he didn't care for? But had she picked up on the fact that, although Jakob respected his wife, he could not say that he worshipped her like other husbands did their wives? He could not or would not pay lip service to such nonsensical comments. Levin never intended to hurt Sara by not letting her into his world, but it was his way to always remain a closed book. He remembered the discomforting, sympathetic look on her face she would sometimes covertly bestow upon him when she sat and watched him read, her lace work in her elegant, productive hands. Jakob wondered if the shades of sadness he sometimes detected in her insightful eyes were borne from pity for her husband. Levin felt a sharp wave of pity for his wife, thinking that he might have pulled her down into the singular gloom and emotional frigidity in which his life was limed. After a few years Sara gave up trying to entwine her limbs in his. Jakob didn't wish his monastic existence on anyone. He couldn't even blame the stress and drama of the apocalyptic times for the dissolution of his marriage. He had been a passionless, dislocated husband – but if love did exist Jakob felt now that there was no one else upon this loveless planet who he loved more, or would wish to express that he cared for. He had been married to the loveliest of wives, but at the same time as possessing this proud, enlightening sensation, Jakob was winged by the poisonous arrows of loss and regret.

Charlotte experienced a momentary dilemma in deciding whether to try to enliven Jakob's mood – or try to sympathise and root out his apparent sorrows.

"And how is the patient this afternoon?"

"Well enough now not to be considered a patient so much," Jakob drily, some might say curtly, replied. His brow became creased, like clouds congregating and congealing upon the horizon.

Charlotte placed the tray on the bedside table and then motioned to plump up Jakob's pillows.

"Please, there is no need, I am comfortable enough."

"Are you sure you are feeling all right, Jakob?"

"I am sure that I am the best judge of how I am feeling. I do not wish to appear rude but I would simply like just to be left alone now, Charlotte. You said yourself how busy it was at the hospital. I do not wish to be an encumbrance which keeps you from your work."

"You are not an encumbrance. Don't be silly."

"But I am keeping you from your work."

"Would you like me to call on you this evening?"

"No, tomorrow will be fine. Thank you for all you help," Jakob said mechanically – and then turned his head away from the nurse, to intimate that their exchange was over.

Charlotte departed from the room, more stung by Jakob's ingratitude than being concerned for his health.

Jakob was left alone with his self-pity, self-condemnation and the spectre of his wife. He later realised that he had treated Charlotte with the same air of condescension that he had often treated Sara with. Had his wife been so selfless and accommodating because that was merely the way she had been conditioned? No, Levin finally realised. He had been patriarchal and dismissive towards Sara because he could be; he had no choice but to be the dominant partner if she was so submissive. How he now wished that just once she would've railed at him, shown some colour; he was not unreasonable. He might have listened and changed. But did she know that, even if she was in the right, Jakob had the ability to win or negate any argument? Philosophy doesn't always make one a better person. Yet, like Charlotte, rather than being a sum of her parts, had Sara made a conscious choice to be so selfless, Christian? In her simple faith and felicity did she experience that higher state of consciousness that Jakob had often read about, but never responded to or had reason to believe in? Faith was a delusion. A leap was tantamount to a fall. Couldn't altruism be explained as a socio-biological phenomenon, present in other species in nature? Is romantic love not a matter of bio-chemistry – or a cultural construct? But yet did he not love his wife? Levin was plunged into the mire of doubting his doubts. At the same time as feeling that the walls were closing in on him his thoughts were spinning out webs in all directions, enmeshed in contradictory layers of morbid introspection. He finally found respite and gained a semblance of control by reducing it back to his life-view that he knew nothing and that one should act 'as if' there were a God. Yes, that was his official line when he had taught at the university, but finally, consumed by an awful, inexplicable spirit, Levin returned to his excruciating despair. His life was drenched in sin and guilt. The feverish Jew scrunched up his bedclothes in his fists, his black eyes moistened and the cultural construct of God became a reality, all but physically present in the room with him. Gripping him. Judging him. A more rational Jakob would later put the ordeal down to a return of an old nervous disorder.

*

As much as Charlotte felt a desire to see the captain again before she went back to the hospital, she decided to leave a note for him. She was a little distraught after seeing Jakob and she would have felt strange waiting or searching the house for him, although she dearly wished to thank the captain and apologise again. She left the note with a kindly but slightly backward maid and walked towards the front door. As she did so however Charlotte felt a chill down her spine - a presentiment of the frenzied destruction that the house and its beautiful interiors might suffer at the hands of the Russian army. The pale-faced nurse felt a shard of remorse as she replayed in her mind her comment about hoping that the Russians would have as much respect for Herr Fischer as she did. Despite her interest in the captain and concern for Jakob, Charlotte wished for no more now than just to leave the household and return to her normal routine. So poorly lit was the arched passage that, as Charlotte began to open the door, the crack of sunlight from outside shone like an ingot of gold.

"You are leaving, Miss Friedrich?"

"Yes. I left a note with one of your maids," Charlotte said, finding herself staring as she took in the contrary and attractive figure descending the stairs. It was as much as a pleasure as it was a surprise to find the captain dressed in an elegant navy blue summer suit instead of his uniform. So too he was casually wearing his shirt without a tie, his undone top button revealing his neck and the top of his chest. She blushed.

"I gather you have checked upon Jakob? Is he feeling any better? Does he, or you, need anything?"

"Jakob remarked that he was fine. He felt well enough to dismiss me, if that's a good sign. He said he wanted to be left alone for the afternoon."

"Will you do me the honour of having lunch with me, Miss

Friedrich?" Robert amiably asked, "It is the very least I can do to thank you for everything."

The young nurse hesitated, partly because her inexperienced heart skipped a beat.

"That would be lovely, thank you," Charlotte politely replied, trying to suppress the tide of feelings ebbing into her breast. Charlotte didn't quite know what to feel – or what she was feeling. Any apprehension she felt suddenly melted like snow however. She shut the door, smoothed out her dress and followed her host through to the smaller of his two dining rooms. Butterflies fluttered in her stomach. When the officer's back was turned Charlotte briefly closed her eyes – to either revel in or temper her sensations – and thought how she would have a story to tell her cousin Eva that evening.

CHAPTER EIGHTEEN

"Goodbye, Miss Friedrich."

"Goodbye, Captain," Charlotte replied – the light and wine still gleaming in her eyes from the memorable afternoon.

"You will be visiting us again I hope? To check up on Jakob."

"I promised Jakob that I would call on him tomorrow, if that's fine for you, Captain?"

"My only condition is that you begin to call me Robert. I have never really taken to the title of captain, neither has it much taken to me I suspect."

"I shall hopefully see you tomorrow then, Robert," she replied, smiling again, abashed yet happy.

Charlotte left late afternoon, a warm vermillion sun still melting the clouds like butter in a pan. She felt like a teenager (a state of being she had rarely experienced in her teens). Robert had kindly offered to drive Charlotte home but she wanted to visit the hospital. The young woman was not quite dizzy enough not to realise that her head was spinning, so she thought it prudent to get a dose of fresh air and normality. Charlotte did not consider the captain to be anything but a would-be friend; they had parted not with him gallantly kissing her hand but with a handshake, nor did she dare presume that she now meant anything to the officer. But the pretty smile on her face betrayed the bloom which was beginning to unfold within her heart. He had got under her skin for one reason or another. No sooner had she left than Charlotte began to gladly replay in her mind her scenes with the officer, his words and expressions, how when he smiled broadly or laughed his eyes would soften and he would shyly cover up his mouth with his hand, as if he were ashamed or uncomfortable at displaying such open emotion.

Charlotte remembered the force and sincerity of the Captain's confession, "I am more of a sinner than sinned against, Miss Friedrich. But please believe me when I say that I did not know the extent of Jakob's condition and mistreatment. No, I should not plead ignorance."

Charlotte observed the self-inflicted torment in the captain's features and her heart went out to him as if she was a young girl again and Robert was a broken-winged bird. The nurse's maternal instincts unlaced their loosely-tied bodice and, like she would with one of her ailing patients, Charlotte placed one of her hands on his as she sat opposite to the tortured officer over the dining table.

"If you are not to blame, then you shouldn't punish yourself."

In one hand the officer reciprocated the tender grasp of Charlotte, but in the other Robert tensely grasped the handle of his knife. His usually strong and healthy countenance appeared strained and feverish, his eyes glowering at himself. Charlotte both feared and pitied his intense, crisis-ridden aspect. Later on that night, sleepless, alone with her dream-like thoughts, Charlotte would think of Captain Fischer in terms of Milton's Satan – defiant in the face of a God that, although he believes in Him, he cannot serve. The captain was a tragic – more than a romantic – hero. And she felt proud, privileged, that only she seemed to know what he was really like – and how much goodness he was capable of.

"He above the rest
In shape and gesture stood proudly eminent,
A fairer person lost not heav'n."

Robert suddenly took his hand back and recoiled, conscious of the pathetic figure he was cutting – and the mawkish look on the nurse's face. He took possession of himself again and realised how much of a cliché and character from a Russian novel he was becoming, or had become. Fischer smiled to himself, easing the tension in his features and thoughts.

"I warrant I have been reading too much Shakespeare, Charlotte. My life is far from as dramatic as I sometimes think it is. I fear that if I were a character from Shakespeare it would be one from a comedy, not tragedy. Gratiano perhaps, a figure who 'speaks an infinite deal of nothing, his reasons are as two grains of sand hidden in two bushels of wheat; you shall seek all day ere you find them, and when you find them, they are not worth the search'," Robert posited, his wry manner returning.

Charlotte recognised that Robert was attempting to alter the tone and subject of the conversation. She offered him a knowing, sympathetic smile to convey her understanding.

Robert was relieved to see the maid enter with a basket of bread rolls; the interlude gave the arch-actor some time to re-group. As if nothing had happened, or been said, Robert asked, whilst the maid was leaving, "So tell me Charlotte, what made you decide to become a nurse?"

"After visiting the hospital, I felt that I had little choice… Because I could help out, I believed that I should. What made you want to join the army, Captain, if you do not mind me asking? From the looks of things you have little need of the money from the pay."

Robert gave the most honest answer he could by shrugging his shoulders and smiling, whimsically, "I don't know. It kills time?"

"I fear that the times will kill us first," Charlotte dolefully replied, troubled. Robert's features too sank in a brief, pained expression. But he revived upon feeling the gentle touch of her soft fingertips upon the back of his hand. Staring at him with unaffected sympathy and charm, wise beyond her years, Charlotte brushed her hair out of her pretty eyes with her other hand and tucked it behind her ears. Robert would later question – was her concern real? Had her faith known despair? Were those equitable glances now becoming amorous? – Interrogating his own feelings as much as the girl's.

"The Evil one abstracted stood
From his own evil, and for a time remained
Stupidly good, of emnity disarmed."

Robert Fischer was far less giddy or hormonal when parting from Charlotte – and he had drunk a bottle of Chardonnay. His thoughts turned to the fate of Jakob. Fully aware that it was but a conceit, the increasingly spiritualised German attached himself to the belief that if he somehow could save Jakob, he would be saving himself.

*

Night descended, sombre as a funeral. Jakob was awake, sitting upright and blankly staring at the wall, ignoring the throbbing in the back of his spindly leg. A half-eaten meal and book lay on the bed next to him. So absorbed was he in his thoughts that Jakob failed to notice the captain appear before him. Robert could not tell whether Jakob looked better or worse but he did look a little different, diffident.

"Charlotte has not long left. She said she would try to come back tomorrow," Robert opened to break the ice, his voice treading on egg shells.

"I should really apologise to her. I think I might have been short or ungrateful towards her this afternoon."

Jakob still owned a detached look on his face and talked as if he were holding a conversation with himself as well as with the other person in the room.

"I am ready to return to my work, Captain. I imagine that you would also like your room back."

"You're perfectly welcome to stay in here, Jakob. I neither consider this room, or this house, my home."

"Where do you consider home, if you do not mind me asking?"

Robert shrugged his shoulders.

"Nowhere."

"What do you care about Captain, or believe in?" Jakob asked, narrowing his eyes in concentration as though he was being reflective more than inquisitive. The question was sudden, dramatic, intrusive.

"My apathy?" the officer replied, wrinkling up his face in a humorous expression. Robert's cheerful, enlightened indifference helped stir Jakob from his vacancy. He couldn't help raise a corner of his mouth at the Captain's answer.

"If I am honest I cannot say that I believe in anything, nor do I truly care about anything. What is it to care, or believe for real? There is no causal argument for belief. Logic, mathematical logic, rings true, but can a man believe in or care about logic? Does logic care about us? Yet logic and my reason cannot, will not, permit me to put my faith in something that is ultimately contingent."

The German officer shrugged his shoulders again as if to intimate that he was happily ignorant of his argument and attitude. But yet more than the argument Robert sympathised with the defiance and despair in Jakob's strained, ghostly features, for had not his own despair and defiance manifested itself in similar philosophical and nihilistic outbursts? *If God is dead then all is lawful.*

"You should have faith in your ability as a translator. I have been reading your work."

It was now Jakob's turn to shrug his shoulders.

"I do not really know if you can call it my work captain, but I would like to return to my duties. It keeps my mind occupied."

"If you must insist on returning to work then let me insist that you keep this room. There is a bell there that runs down into the pantry. If you ring it a maid should attend to you within minutes. As much as I have used it in the past, I dare say that it still works."

"Thank you."

Jakob bowed his head in pensive thought and fiddled with his hands, pausing.

"I would ask a favour of you, Captain, also. Could you find out what has happened to my wife, Sara?"

Robert was here reminded of the guilt and shame of his past actions, his old self. He was struck also by the dread of the future, trying to explain what he imagined had been his wife's fate.

"You should know Jakob that it was not my decision to forbid you contact with your wife."

"I suspected that, Captain."

"I'll do my best, but I cannot promise anything."

"I would ask also if you could find out about a friend of mine, Karl Friedrich, Charlotte's father. She told me that he disappeared some years ago after helping some people get out of the country."

"It is the least I can do."

Before the pause had an opportunity to become pregnant with

awkwardness, Robert noticed the book upon the bed.

"What are you reading?"

"I remember enjoying it when I was young – and I needed to take my mind off things. You have an extensive library."

Jakob leaned over and passed the lovingly preserved leather bound book to the officer.

Robert took the book in his hands and read the title out loud with a sumptuous grin plastered on his attractive face, as if he were sharing a private joke.

"*In Praise of Folly.*"

CHAPTER NINETEEN

Time passes.

Jakob's condition suitably improved and he became capable of hobbling around and taking advantage of a certain amount of freedom and independence within the household. The servants were still apprehensive of interacting with the prisoner but Charlotte continued to visit Jakob. If she was honest the good-hearted girl would have conceded that the house held a greater attraction in the form of its owner. For even though Charlotte spent considerably more of her time in the company of her former tutor it was the human jigsaw of the captain who was often the topic of conversation and her private thoughts.

For a week or so after their first meeting Robert took time out to get to know the nurse and make sure that she felt comfortable calling in on the house and her patient. They lunched and took walks together in the nearby park, exchanged books and traded witticisms. However the captain soon became occupied with certain business matters and was unable to spare much time for the young, engaging nurse. A mature and responsible Robert also felt uneasy with the potential scenario that she might become attracted to him; he noticed the way Charlotte sometimes looked at him – and conversely the way he sometimes gazed at her when she wasn't looking. Robert did not now own the time or will to seduce the fair and innocent girl; he was too old for her and was content just to remain friends with the well-read, spirited nurse.

However, in the space that Robert afforded the starry-eyed girl, she was able to paint such romanticised pictures of the captain that her affection increased rather than diminished; Robert's slight discomfort and lack of intimacy around Charlotte only made her more eager to prove to him that he had no reason to feel awkward in her company.

The cheery middle-aged housekeeper, with stubby fingers shaped like sausages, took the nurse up to the prisoner's room again. As much as Charlotte had developed a soft spot for Frau Huber she could have died with shame one afternoon when, on encountering Robert in the passage, the housekeeper said to her master, "Doesn't Miss Friedrich look pretty today?"

Frau Huber left the chamber immediately after opening the door of the room to the nurse, her sense of dotage not quite stretching to the Jewish prisoner yet. Without taking the time to even greet Jakob, Charlotte unassumingly asked, with not a little disappointment puncturing her tone, "Is the captain not in today then?"

"Morning Charlotte. You're early."

"I have a few free hours before I start my shift. I thought I'd see how you are."

"The captain informed me that he would be out for most of the day I'm afraid, on business I presume."

"What do you think of the captain?" Charlotte innocently asked. Jakob had been expecting the question for some time. He more so than the nurse, or Robert even, was conscious of the growing infatuation. Out of a duty to her and also her father, Jakob felt he needed to caution Charlotte to be guarded against the womanising officer and not make him out to be something he was not. In his solemn monotone voice Jakob offered his rehearsed reply:

"The Captain suffers from the malady of being able to find irony in everything he encounters in the world, yet he is far more sensitive and grave than his humour sometimes suggests. He also values his privacy. I can see how you might find him handsome, or intriguing, but be careful, Charlotte, not to speculate on the captain too much so as to lose sight of him, or more importantly yourself," Jakob carefully posited, sounding somewhat like the girl's lecturer again.

"Oh no, it's nothing like that!" Charlotte nervously laughed and answered whilst blushing violently and lowering her head, "I just wonder what the captain will do after the war. Do you think he will resign from the army?" The observant nurse once noticed how he frequently adjusted his uniform in discomfort. The sensitive girl took this to mean how unhappy Robert was in wearing the uniform and being an officer, albeit if the truth be told the jacket and trousers had shrunk due to a new laundry woman incorrectly washing and pressing the garments that afternoon.

"The Captain is uncommonly wealthy, he is free to do whatever he wishes after the war," Jakob said, pretending not to notice Charlotte's increasing crimsoning cheeks.

"He didn't make his fortune from the war, did he?"

"I do not believe so. He is from a wealthy family but, in more ways than one, the captain is largely a self-made man. I also believe he is a prominent patron of your hospital, no?"

"And the hospital is not the only charity that Robert gives generously to."

"Do you intend to continue working in the hospital after the war?"

"I suppose so. I also intend to try and get in contact with Papa after the war. What will you do after all this is over Jakob?"

"I must try to find my wife, Sara," Jakob replied, with more conviction in his voice to do so than hope for any success.

"I remember your wife, she was lovely. She used to spoil my cousin and I, and treat us – and make us promise not to tell you."

Jakob smiled wistfully, then wanly. Sara was good with children; she was always willing to play the surrogate aunt to the neighbour's infants. She came alive in the company of children and lost the sobriety she had when she was with him. Although he did not always appreciate his wife then, Jakob played back memories and scenes of Sara glowing as she cradled his niece in her arms - and how she would produce a chocolate bar or toy car from nowhere to a neighbourhood child she had never met before. He pictured himself too in the scene. Occasionally he would gaze upon her fondly, or more often than not he would frown with disapproval, thinking that she might be spoiling the pupil who he had to maintain a professional relationship with. But the warmth of these scenes could not redeem his past frigidity. By being forever surrounded by other people's children Jakob had reasoned that any maternal desires in Sara were satiated. She never mentioned or complained about not having children with him. So too Levin vowed that, as an act of revenge and polemic against this world, he would not bring a child into its wastelands and prisons. But he conceded that this was but a conceit to justify his selfishness. Jakob began to clinically look upon himself ten years ago and saw a garlanded Professor of English and Philosophy who could deliver marathon lectures on Hegel, but not convey to his wife that he cared for her; he spoke four languages, but seldom spoke to anyone – believing most conversations to be either tautologous or oxymoronic. Another conceit Jakob would remember formulating was promising himself that he would be as indifferent to the world as the world was to him.

CHAPTER TWENTY

They made an odd couple. Christian was now a deserter living with Wolfgang in his friend's cramped apartment. He had let his hair and beard grow but, as Christian never ventured outside for fear of an improbable capture, the former soldier had no need of his suspicious change of appearance. Christian spent his time daily and dully dreaming of an end to the war – even if it meant defeat – and drinking bottles of acidic wine. He sometimes read over, when asked, some of Wolfgang's pamphlets and speeches but most of the time the soldier buried his head in the sand – or in a bottle – and sat in one of the apartment's two chairs (which also doubled up as his bed) listening to whatever was cackling on the radio.

Wolfgang increasingly seethed and ground his teeth at his new lodger but nevertheless openly tolerated his unwelcome friend. The house proud Nazi made it worse for himself by amplifying Christian's annoying habits (such as breathing heavily through his nose when eating and not leaving the newspaper the way he found it). He dwelt on his loss of privacy and freedom. But nevertheless Wolfgang tolerated his friend, for after all he was paying him for the displeasure. Wolfgang would be averse to admit it, especially to himself, but he was also a little scared and intimidated by his new housemate. The asinine soldier was physically superior to the old man, even with just with one hand at his disposal. Yet Wolfgang comforted himself with the fact that he was the dolt's intellectual and moral superior. He was as resourceful as Christian was strong and the deserter needed him more than he needed the deserter. Wolfgang also appreciated Christian in that the rent money he gave him financed the party activist's printing costs.

One such article which Wolfgang intended to print was a speech that he was composing for one of the now poorly attended, spasmodic forums held down at the town's main National Socialist's club. Hunched over his desk, with a pair of half-moon glasses perched on his nose that he had stolen from one of his Jewish neighbours years ago, Wolfgang began to read over to himself part of the second draft of his rallying speech.

"...I witness now more than ever a united Europe under the gaze of one eagle, his eyes as keen as his talons. I still see a Europe united in policy, emblem, in currency and, when war achieves it, a Europe united by peace. Why do I see it? Because it is inevitable. The train has yet to pull into the station, but the tracks are being laid and there is such steam left in the engine that hell itself, as well as heaven, is on our side. Throw not your tickets away brothers, for those not on board will be stranded.

Yet I would throw my ticket away if it meant that my brother and my brother's children reached our destination. A fool would he be also to leap off of a speeding train, especially when we are past the point of no return. Aye, we are more than half way there. Has not the Jewish cancer been eradicated which weakened us for so long? Has not the vermin been exterminated? I see a Europe united by a history and culture doing battle not internally but joining forces to be a, the, world power.

I see here faces in front of me emanating strength, will and honour. Each child now in a German womb is wholly superior; let us create a world for him worthy of his race. The most dangerous thing for us to do is cut off the process of natural selection; we must not resist scientific and economic truth; we must not maintain the weak at the expense of the healthy. When selflessness is unnatural it is a sin. Let us embrace science, natural selection, serve it so that it may provide us with children who are worthy of Gods; science is our race's birth right."

Wolfgang paused for a moment and calmly sipped some cloudy water from an even cloudier glass. He briefly looked behind him at a Christian who was clumsily attempting to fish a hair out from his tumbler of wine. The malignant pamphleteer shook his head in condescension and disgust. He took another sip of water, recapped on a few things – the inflexions in his voice, the pauses and when to harden one's eyes in determination and sincerity – and read on.

"I can envision a Europe free from the parasite of the Jew, a Europe of one voice, one police force and one language; but now our vision must be realised. It was a struggle to cure us from the sickness of the Jew, but have we not lanced the infection? Yes it was a struggle, but the idea of struggle is as old as life itself. In this struggle the stronger, the more able, win – while the less able, the weak, falter. Struggle is the father of all things, my brothers. In a year, two years, however long it takes – destiny runs by no clock – our children will remember our struggle and eat of the fruits of our victory.

But to eat of the fruits of victory we must first plant the seeds; and the Russian, the irreligious Bolshevik, is soiling our land. How do we sterilise this wound? We fight! We fight with kultar. We must heat our blood till it burns anyone, anything, standing in our way. A ring of fire must surround each man, town and border."

Wolfgang took another sip of water and witnessed a Christian transfixed by the remaining drops of wine plopping out of the brown bottle and into his glass. The glazed look in his eyes betrayed that he was more drunk than sober. Anytime soon Wolfgang would expect his friend to become both irritable and irritating. At such a time Wolfgang would have easily swapped the pride of feeling superior to the oaf for some peace and quiet and his little world back.

"I am out of wine," Christian moaned, pleading and whinging like a child.

Wolfgang ignored his companion and hoped that his silence would provide the answer to the request inherent in his statement.

"Wolfgang, we are out of wine. Are you going to go out and get some more?"

"I'm working. Why don't you go out and get some more?" the national socialist wearily replied with his back to his friend.

"You know why I can't go out, you idiot. Someone might see me."

"Don't be so paranoid."

"You'd be paranoid in my position."

"Why do you always say 'in my position' instead of being honest and saying that you are a deserter?"

Wolfgang stated this with relish and hoped that it would force his friend to cower in shame and, more importantly, in silence. Yet Christian was now as sullen and uninhibited as a drunk perturbed by the thought of where his next drink was coming from.

"Are you calling me a coward?" Christian ejaculated, following his demanding question with a hiccup.

With his back still rudely pointed towards his uncouth tenant Wolfgang drily replied, "No, I am calling you a deserter."

As well prepared as Wolfgang was with this comment Christian too, this time, was equally prepared in his response. He would have the last word this time in this round of routine quarrelling. Christian's sleepless night the evening before had been partly due to him thinking up arguments and criticisms to cut the supercilious old man down to size. Who was he to talk down to him?

"If there is a coward in this room it's not me. Have your 'eternal flames of revenge' gone out? Have natural causes got to the captain before your – what was it? – 'Jove-like vengeance'? If I make you sick by being a deserter, you make me laugh. There is no evil that you have not committed."

Wolfgang immediately flushed and snarled internally. He briefly recalled the bombastic speech he gave to save face after his humiliation at the hands of the arrogant 'pretty-boy' captain. Time had passed but it had not healed his wounded pride concerning the disastrous episode. How his beady eyes had blazed with rage, how he had spat curses into the air, swearing revenge. He had pictured the captain and other officers laughing at his expense behind his back. He still frequently replayed the scene over in his head but the ideal outcomes were so divorced from reality that it only served to rub the itch; equally, or most of all, Wolfgang dwelt upon the fact that it was a snivelling Jew who had proved to be the cause of his miseries, the thorn in his flesh that only vengeance could remove. Christian here, however much he grated upon his mood, was but a Chorus to the frustrations he felt, not the author of them.

"Not got nothing to say now, have you?" the bullish deserter added.

Calm, determined and resigned to it Wolfgang remarked, "The Jew and that Captain will be dead before the end of the month."

Up until now Christian had doubted Wolfgang's sincerity in terms of his revenge. Living with the fascist day to day had quickly eroded the amount of respect and comradeship he had once possessed for the original Party member. He had seen the philosopher naked, quite literally, warts and all. He had twigs for arms and legs – as chalky as Danish Blue cheese, replete with pronounced veins. He was also mean as well as mean-spirited; his tea was so weak as to be barely describable as such and the bread he bought was hard enough to hammer a nail into the wall with. Whenever Christian made himself something to eat he could feel the niggard's frowning eyes burning a hole in his back, monitoring what he ate and doing the math in terms of how much board money his tenant had given him. Christian found himself biting his tongue in the presence of the armchair politician and commander. He possessed a blind faith in the Fuhrer, blaming his incompetent and cowardly deputies for his defeats and errors in judgement. And how dare he admonish Rommel! The draft-dodger (through the excuse of his temperamental leg injury) wasn't even fit to say his name. Christian admonished himself also though – how he had stupidly lapped up the speechmaker's anecdotes and propaganda in the tavern, qualifying and deepening his anti-Semitism. But Wolfgang was but a bitter, un-heroic, selfish codger with more of his dreary, lonely life behind him than in front of him. What had this activist actually done? Christian increasingly came to the conclusion that he didn't want to end up like the old curmudgeon. But now, here, Wolfgang had committed himself to action, sounding like the prophetic voice of one of his pamphlets. Could these be just words, or did the prattling National Socialist really intend to murder the captain?

CHAPTER TWENTY-ONE

Part of Robert's energies of late had been devoted to the task of honouring the requests made to him by Jakob; that of divining the fates of his wife and Charlotte's father. His influence – the unspoken sway of powerful friends and certain bribes – had greased the wheels and finally the determined Captain received the answers to his inquiries not two hours from each other, but answers which were a world apart. The melancholic German closed his eyes and sighed outside Jakob's bedroom before he knocked and entered. Jakob was just finishing reading over a poem he had translated. The author was one Edward Middlesex, a nineteenth century Romantic poet. In the introduction to the volume the editor had argued how much the poet had been under-appreciated in his lifetime. Despite his obscurity and failure however, Jakob dryly argued that he had still not been under-appreciated enough. Or perhaps he was being too harsh.

"As the moon charms the sea,
As the bloom charms the bee,
Mary Clement so charms the breeze

With a song so divine,
So melodic and fine,
The birds are mute upon the trees.

Fortunate he must be
To draw such notes from she
Who would Heaven's choir so make.
A Captain is John Dale,
Missing for two years now.
And her heart pines, but does not break.

Tears from your eyes would stream,
Unpick would your heart's seam,
Should you clement Mary's song hear,
With dejection unfurled.
Seduced into her world
You would be, entertained but drear.

And she is as beautiful
As her song's sorrowful.
I pine for her, but she mourns him.
If I were wedded not
I would, with her, tie the knot.
Such a waste of beauty's a sin."

Jakob shifted his inexpressive gaze towards the captain when
he entered but then commenced to read again and finish the

sentence he was working on.

"I apologise for disturbing you Jakob, but I thought that I should tell you as soon as I found out. I have just been on the telephone with a contact in the Ministry. I'm sorry Jakob."

The officer's words and tone were not and could not be married to the depth and significance of their import - yet Robert's eyes expressed such sympathy for once that they were like two outstretched hands, ready to catch Jakob's tears. But the widower had already buried his chin into his chest. He did not want to look at the captain and that uniform.

"Would you like to be left alone?"

"You are responsible for this (Levin could not bring himself to say 'my wife's death'). You're despicable. Everybody is, even those who are not even born yet. We are all Nazis. It is our original sin. The first sin is the denial of sin. When God made Man they say he could afford to rest. He should've rested earlier," Jakob tartly exclaimed, his face a sneer.

The gentle Jew's usually soft, logical voice faltered, as did the cadence of his breathing and pulse. Jakob suddenly became animated, striped with underlining resentment and despair. It was as if someone had chucked a giant rock into his oasis of calm. Yet still one could trace the strain in the widower's face to remain suppressed, as if he were an epileptic trying to soberly master the stirrings of a fit. But fissures appeared in the glass.

"My cat was poisoned by boys no older than twelve who two years before my wife had given Christmas gifts to. A colleague of mine, a Professor of Physics who served as a medical orderly in the Great War, was shot in the head because he complained to a drunken corporal that his hands were too large to fit inside a drainage pipe to clean away the excrement. I had to bury his body with numb, blood-soaked hands. The blood was caked under my fingernails for a week (Jakob here examined his fingers as if he could still see the stains). My wife has been spat in the face at and molested before my eyes. My brother had his gold tooth pulled in the camp in order to bribe a private and receive a loaf of bread for his family. Where does the hate come from? You are a student of hate, Captain. Or have you just become enslaved by the triumph and vanity of being the Master Race? There must be a morning after to this Bacchic orgy, to this butchery and fanatical ignorance. The state was created to serve Man, Man was not formed to serve the state. My home, job, possessions, rights, freedoms have been taken away from me. You have become a law unto yourselves. We have been demonised and dehumanised by inhuman devils. If I had a prayer for God it would be that I would hope he wasn't a merciful being."

Choking upon tears which welled in his dark eyes – his measured voice now raspy with desperation – Levin closed his speech and lowered his head again, partly in embarrassment at his emotional outburst.

Robert, unable to deal with the scene and thinking it best to do as Jakob asked, motioned to leave after a swollen pause. Yet as he got to the door Jakob, reining in a certain composure, spoke to the German.

"Have you received any news concerning Charlotte's father?"

"Yes, apparently he escaped into England. He is now wanted by the state."

As much as a solitary grain of sand removed from the hourglass will alter the time, Jakob's expression nevertheless betrayed the speculation of consolation.

"Could you tell Charlotte? She said that she might visit this afternoon. I would prefer to be left alone for the rest of the day, Captain, if that's fine by you?"

"Of course, I understand. If you need anything, just ask," Robert kindly replied and attempted a cordial, consoling smile which was almost pathetic in its execution. The captain left with anger stuck in his throat for the German – and pity in his heart for the Jew. No, it was fury and pity in relation towards all men.

His breathing still irregular, like the tick-tock of a broken metronome, Jakob continued to glare at the wall. The alms of sleep had even abandoned him. Levin couldn't even bring himself to work. He couldn't regain the mood which had become second nature to him over the years. His pen felt heavy, like a murder weapon.

*

Her skin was as emollient as a peach, her hair let down – pouring like blonde sunshine over her shoulders and back. Rain freckled the air and her face. Charlotte stood upon the steps and pressed the bell. Her question as to whether Robert was at home or not was soon answered, for it was the captain himself who opened the door and greeted Charlotte with a friendly enough smile. But there was something wrong, or rather not right, she intuited as only a young woman can, or cares to.

"Afternoon Charlotte, please come in."

The handsome officer politely held the door open for the nurse – who was still in her uniform – and allowed her to pass through under his arm.

"Unfortunately you will be unable to see Jakob today. He doesn't wish to be disturbed. Don't be too alarmed, he is in fine health, but please do not ask me to say anymore."

"Would you like me to come back tomorrow then?"

"No, please, stay awhile Charlotte. I have some news concerning you."

Charlotte was immediately and immensely engaged by the fact that he would concern himself with her. What could he want with her?

Robert found himself dumbly staring at Charlotte again. Only for a moment, but yet a moment nonetheless, Robert envisioned the elation and authentic, glistening emotion that might soon animate that youthful face which grew prettier and prettier on each viewing. As he hypnotically gazed at the girl, as she took off the watch pinned upon her breast, Robert noticed what small and delicate ivory hands she had. He realised how that whenever he saw Charlotte he noticed something fresh and admirable about her – and not just in terms of the girl's physical charms.

"There is nothing to be too worried about Miss Friedrich. Please, come through."

Robert Fischer and Charlotte Friedrich entered the parlour,

which looked out onto a well-kept garden; every blade of grass and shrub had been planted with surgical precision by a green-fingered Abraham Solomon and his wife, but yet the garden still owned a natural, vital air. The lawn was trim and glistening with dew. Bluebells, cowslip and blood red pansies hemmed in the square carpet of grass. A small fish pond sat in the shade of a couple of pear trees, whose branches had grown and stretched out to now touch and support each other – seemingly holding hands like an old married couple. But, as crisp and verdant as the garden appeared, Robert could not take his eyes off of the radiance of Charlotte's beautiful aspect and fine hair in the ebullient sunshine; like the small vista outside, the girl was Nature perfected – Robert would later muse.

"Jakob asked a favour of me some time ago, Charlotte. He asked me to investigate the fate and whereabouts of a friend of his, Karl Friedrich. He is wanted by the authorities, but I'm pleased to say that he is alive and well and living in England."

Tears, relief and unvarnished joy naturally bloomed from Charlotte's features. She appeared as overwhelmed and redolent as a bride. It was as if Robert had saved her father's life – or her own.

If it had been anyone else but the officer then she might have embraced them (with Robert being of course the one person in all the world, bar her father, who Charlotte would have most wished to lean on right now – and have him lean on her) but the wonderfully shy girl had no need to express her happiness, her happiness was enough.

"Would you like to be left alone for a while?"

"No, please stay. I'm sorry," Charlotte pleaded, wiping away another bejewelled tear.

The pause consisting of Robert admiring God knows what about Charlotte and the nurse becoming self-conscious of how emotional she must have been appearing was broken by the Captain offering the nurse his handkerchief. As he did so Charlotte squeezed his hand.

"This means the world to me. I was starting to lose faith. How can I thank you?" she issued, punctuated by sobs.

The seducer had experienced the power and charm of human touch before, indeed true seduction cannot take place without the percussion of its sensation (one must time its execution to perfection of course, naturally) – but Robert had always been the conductor. Now these were a woman's fingers upon his heartstrings. Was the seducer being seduced? Emotion must be suppressed until the point where it cannot help but seep out, like puss he had once joked, half-seriously, to his friend and lawyer Jorge Albetz.

"The look upon your face is reward enough. I've never been one to make people happy. I could get used to it, though," Robert amiably replied.

"You are too kind. I can only imagine what kind of picture I am making now."

Charlotte spluttered out a laugh mixed with a sob and dried her eyes again. She thought it fortunate that, being already flushed somewhat, her blushes were concealed.

"It's a picture that I shall hang in my memory forever," Robert gently expressed.

Gentleness ousted the cloud which usually hung over him. At heart, he was a gentleman. Charlotte realised that she could love the reality of Robert more than the fantasy of all the literary heroes she adored in her youth. He was every girl's dream, handsome and witty, and rich (but this last and by no means insubstantial virtue Charlotte listed not as one of Robert's virtues).

The romantic girl dried the last of her sparkling tears and offered to return Robert's handkerchief.

"Please, keep it," he smiled and kindly pressed the silk handkerchief back into the grateful girl's hands.

The arch-womaniser employed a seduction technique but I honestly believe that he owned no intention to seduce Charlotte in such a calculated, carnal vein. The technique was the same, but not the scene. In the immediacy of the moment, with Charlotte resplendent with femininity and personality, Robert sincerely loved his Ophelia. He was possessed by a refined rather than circadian spirit. How could he have not desired to kiss those tear-soaked lips that glistered full and ripe even without make-up? He was torn. Yet he succumbed, telling himself that it was what she wanted too. He was doing it for her.

And so Robert momentarily focused his eyes upon Charlotte's face and raised his mouth in a boyish, infectious smirk, as if he were smiling to himself at something privately humorous.

"What?"

"You have an eyelash upon your chin."

Charlotte smiled bashfully and rubbed her hand across her chin.

"Is it gone?"

"No. Here, let me."

Robert then, in a smooth and tender moment, moved towards Charlotte and lightly stroked his thumb upon her petal-soft chin. Towering above her somewhat he raised the girl's face so that her eyes met his – those eyes charged with gallantry and a glint of dark desire. Charlotte's cool aspect melted from the heat and she lost herself for a moment, but yet her conscious mind still lapped up a thousand thoughts and sensations in a smouldering blur.

A split second after Charlotte's tongue woke up, hungry, she recoiled from the officer and stared at him as if it were a stranger who had just kissed her with such passion and method. No sooner had Charlotte lost herself in the unfamiliar embrace when her shadow shot out a hand and dragged her back from the cliff's edge.

As shaken as Charlotte was - all fire and ice - the amorous captain just as much as the derailed nurse wore a look of shock and anxiety upon his face. He looked pale, mortified – as if he had just discovered that he had committed a crime.

"I'm sorry. I – " the usually self-confident officer stammered.

"No, there is no need. I – " Charlotte interrupted and then broke off.

The pair coyly hung their heads in shame – awkward, messy.

"I should be going now. I have another shift at the hospital," Charlotte said as if nothing had happened, lying. The scene between the pair was both painful and comic to view.

"Please, allow me to show you out," he politely and formally replied.

"No please, there is no need. I know my way. I'll be fine."

Before the captain could say anything else though he was abruptly cut off by the clamour of something smashing against one of the conservatory's glass doors. He soon realised that one of the neighbour's children had merely kicked his muddy football over the fence. During the time in which it took him to poke his head outside of the door and witness the culprit's eyes tentatively peering over the fence, Charlotte stole the opportunity to hastily leave, her heart racing as fast as her small feet. Robert returned to the parlour breathing heavily through his nose, snorting – wearing frustration and something else on his brow.

The disturbed captain then marched back out into the garden and picked up the brat's well-worn and much loved football in one hand – that same hand, now splayed over a football like a talon, which had so recently caressed the small of Charlotte's back. Little Ralf Klose, more out of fear for the huge, scowling captain than any sense of contrition for having kicked his ball over the fence again, wore his best repentant expression. The look had never failed to extricate him from punishment before. But the furious officer was not impressed. Not much could have delivered Robert out of his strange, malignant mood now, engulfing him as it did like some razor-toothed, hydra-headed monster.

But yet our Captain still had his wits about him. He offered to mercifully give the ball back to the penitent child. Ralf Klose, not twelve years old, was too young to know the difference between an ironic, malicious grin and favourable smile. Fischer gestured to give the ball back. It was just about to graze the boy's tickling fingertips when he tossed the football up into the air and, quickly removing his pistol, shot it - avenging the unholy sound the ball had made upon his window.

"Now cause some mischief with that," he drolly said after the singed leather pancake landed on the grass.

With the child beginning to blub in the background the officer smiled with a villainous satisfaction and ventured back inside, spitefully pulling a rose off its thorny stem whilst doing so. Robert Fischer was at heart a blackguard, so why shouldn't he act like one? he posed, both disgusted and amused with himself.

Robert locked himself away in his office, either to protect himself from the world, or to protect the world from him. The rain increasingly thrummed upon the window. The greasy sky was pregnant with a storm. His booted feet rested upon the desk. Robert closed his eyes, absorbing the sorcery of Wagner – and swished his fifth measure of cognac around in the glass. Over the brooding storm and stress of the transcendent music the aesthete pensively quoted Byron whilst wearing a drunk's smile upon his febrile countenance. He briefly mused on the irony and vanity of him, thinking himself in sympathy with the poet. For every self that Robert constructed there was a devil, in his own image, whispering and often laughing in his ear. He was all pretence, a charlatan. He wasn't Byron. He was a no one, nothing. He was an actor playing out various parts for the amusement of himself and the world. He knew that such acute self-consciousness was anathema to a sense of identity, contentment, but he still fell prey to dissecting himself. He was his own worst enemy, indeed he was perhaps his only enemy, for Robert egotistically reasoned that no one else was worthy of the role.

> *"I live,*
> *But live to die; and, living, see no thing*
> *To make death hateful, save an innate clinging,*
> *A loathsome, and yet all invincible*
> *Instinct of life, which I abhor, as I*
> *Despise myself, yet cannot overcome –*
> *And so I live. Would that I had never lived."*

But more than playing Byron, Hamlet or Faust, when he had kissed Charlotte, as he sat in the fusty darkness of his study, Robert Fischer realised that he had been Robert Fischer. Or had he? He was that arch-actor who had created that part, self, who was capable of selflessness and fidelity. When could he become that person, not character, who would be able to look himself in the mirror and not see either Tantalus or a vampire's reflection? When could he be, not just play, that good soul who perhaps only can exist as a character in a novel or play, an Alyosha or Jean Valjean? When would he be able to look at himself in the mirror and see Charlotte, completing the picture? But the officer's past eclipsed the present and any idealised future. There would be no happy ending - there never is. A snake can shed its skin, but it remains a snake. But yet in that significant moment when they kissed, was there not a completion in her being? As he drew Charlotte to him did Robert not genuinely feel her heart beating like his? Love, not just the rapture of a crush or the wild flames of desire, glimmered in her eyes. But yet how she had drawn herself away, like a hand from the fire. It seemed as if she was disgusted with herself for yielding so as the seducer recalled the scene himself, reflected in Charlotte's eyes. He sympathised with her revulsion. He was a profligate who had twice been treated for the clap before he was twenty-one; he might as well try and out-run his shadow as be free from his reputation and make-up. Robert figured he could still seduce Charlotte – and it was experience rather than arrogance which bred this confidence – but that kind of love had burnt itself out for the would-be Christian. He possessed an impulse now to cherish Charlotte on her terms, to nurture a normal relationship (whatever that was). He didn't want to create a work of art in contriving a seduction or affair to remember. He wanted something good and true. But though the spirit is willing, the flesh is weak. Thunder growled in the background. The conclusion was reached in a spirit either of honesty or cowardice. *Why must love always be a question of someone submitting? How do other people sweeten the pill of sacrificing one's freedom? To sacrifice one's will equates to losing that which makes us human, all too human. So is love real – or just a dumb show?*

The heavily blinking, flustered Captain gulped down another glass of cognac in one healthy mouthful. The sneer upon his face as it burned his throat inspired a sneer in his thoughts.

She may be Charlotte, but I will not play Werther… Woman, that was

God's second mistake.

As Fischer went to clasp the half-empty bottle to pour another drink he pricked his finger on the sharp point of his letter knife. He switched on his desk lamp to check the extent of the war wound. As he picked up the knife Robert again noticed the initials on the hilt. Ennui and melancholy are far too pretty terms; a toxic sense of guilt scythed through the once stone-hearted officer in a lumber-puncture pain. Abraham Solomon, those phantom apparitions the oblivious officer had witnessed boarding trains, Heiko Heinrich, Maria and the rest of his harem, Jakob, Rebecca, Charlotte and even that fractious and spoiled child next door, all paraded themselves through Robert's haunted mind like some procession of the un-dead. It was as if there was a bony hand inside the sinner's breast, coldly squeezing his heart until that hand became a fist, rinsing his chamber of blood and tears as if it were a sponge.

CHAPTER TWENTY-TWO

As it would prove difficult to fathom the extent of Robert Fischer's attack of angina, so too how do we diagnose the full seriousness of Jakob Levin's nervous breakdown, if indeed he experienced such a thing?

A bull-dog ant, if cut in half, will still live on for a while; the jaws of the head will attempt to bite the tail, whilst the tail will happily sting the head. So too, in quite a different way, Jakob fought to regain possession of his soul. His soul was linked to Sara – and he had lost her. He forced his trembling hand to carry on working. But the act of forgetting oneself cannot occur without the will of remembrance trying to break through the line. His mind flailed like a half-severed limb. Revelations, putting Jakob in an alternative, darker light, crashed like waves upon his crumbling shore. The serenity which he'd lost seemed like a false memory. The once still, distant sun now boiled the foaming ocean and scorched the golden sands. It was like Jakob had just recovered from a coma or amnesia; everything was new, but stillborn. The ground fell from under the feet of the once academic wunderkind, but did not swallow him up. In a sense it was a type of herbism the way in which Jakob lashed down the sails to finish off another polished epigram, albeit he looked defeated. The gaunt, squinting translator read over the fragment again with an apathetic ardour worthy of its composer. A pair of blisters even began to form upon his thumb and bony index finger from where he had been gripping his pen so violently.

"I agree with you
When I buy you gifts
And you say I shouldn't."
But I know too well
That without their spell
You would say I couldn't."

As dry as Jakob's sense of humour used to be he found the piece un-amusing and unfair. The powerful vision of Sara crept in and was cradled in his thoughts again. Unlike most wives she did not adopt the custom of religiously spending her husband's money, nor did she ever employ any wiles to get her way. She never henpecked him. She never offered fashionable and hypocritical opinions on any and everything like some of the wives in their set. When Sara did give her opinion it was always informed and infused with some semblance of a – some might say – Christian morality, Jakob realised. Compassion and forgiveness always took precedent over the demands of populist and political expediency. Was she a dream? She never dyed her hair, wore more make-up or drowned herself in perfume to alter her age or change the way she felt about herself. Even the unseemly episode of the menopause didn't prove a melodrama for the happy Levins; there were no moody histrionics or pointless hysterics. Unlike her coven of frustrated sisters and their tired brow-beaten husbands, plates were never smashed, mother-in-laws were never confided in and unleashed. Beds were slept in and routines kept to. She had the patience of a saint. Jakob often thought how Sara could've passed as German in her looks. Why didn't he at least get her out of the country before it was too late?

Guilt rose up like bile in his throat again, but Jakob somehow knew he would never be able to be sick, purge himself. He thought that if he could close his eyes for long enough he would fall asleep. No. Respite came in the form of a book again, his book. To take his mind off things Levin decided to scrutinise the captain's library. A copy of Hume's 'A Treatise on Human Nature', which the scholar had translated some time ago, naturally attracted his attention. The captain hadn't commented on reading the book before, but Robert had read the book years ago – and whoever recalls the name of a translator? In academic circles the book had heralded the arrival of a talented prospect. Jakob had published the book when just twenty-six years of age, the same age as Hume was when he released the book originally. Great things were expected of J. Levin. The book was now out of print however, and Jakob's sometime richly anticipated projects – a translation of Voltaire's essays and poetry and a biography of Schopenhauer – never materialised. He had got married. No, that wasn't the reason. His commitment to teaching took up too much of his time and energies. No, he couldn't justly use that as a valid excuse, either. But what had the fuss been about originally? Had he not played down his achievement, too? Jakob had not even written the introduction to the book; he had nothing to say for himself and, even if he did construct an argument, no one was perhaps better qualified than Jakob to deconstruct and criticise it. *The thinker needs no one to refute him, he does that himself'* Nietzsche had once written – and Levin had believed in the maxim. *Without contraries there can be no progression,'* Blake had posited. The dialectic was supposed to bring edification, harmony.

Jakob retrieved the well-preserved book from the shelf, taking note of some of the other titles compactly ordered in a row: 'Origin of the Species', 'The Imitation of Christ', 'Mein Kampf', 'Gulliver's Travels' and 'Crime and Punishment'. Initially they appeared not to be stored in any order, either alphabetised or by subject or author, but upon further inspection Jakob realised, reading a couple of the pencilled in dates on the title pages, that the captain's library was ordered according to the chronology of when he had read the book. Levin felt the ageing yet inflexible book in his hands – looking down upon it with mixed feelings – and let the fanning pages flick through his fingers. He then instinctively turned to that page, that quote (which Robert had underlined) which had so directed Jakob's life-view and dereliction for as long as he could remember.

'*...any hypothesis, that pretends to discover the ultimate original qualities of human nature, ought at first to be rejected as presumptuous and chimerical.'*

Jakob continued to avidly skim through the book, checking to see if the captain had highlighted any other passages. He found the following:

'When I look abroad, I foresee on every side, dispute, contradiction, anger, calumny and detraction. When I turn my eye inward, I find nothing but doubt and ignorance. All the world conspires to oppose and contradict me.'

'Morality, therefore, is more properly felt than judged of.'

'We must look within to find the moral quality.'

Certainly if not contradictory, the juxtaposition of these passages aroused Jakob's black, blunt eyebrow. First of all the critical analyst was surprised at the number of times Hume had punctured his writing with 'I', a fact that he had not noticed so stringently before. There should be no 'I' in philosophy. Jakob's faith in Hume's scepticism, or rather Hume, seemed to recede, like an autumnal leaf curling slipper-like back on itself, before his very eyes. In so many accounts of Hume's character it was written how veritably sanguine the man was, but how can one have been so cheerful knowing what he knew? Had he too been passion's slave? Hume's fork stabbed deep, *'Either our actions are determined, in which case we are not responsible for them, or they are the results of random events, in which case we are not responsible for them'.*

Sweat glazed his brow. Ink stained his fingers. His expression seemed either pained or sceptical – or both. Apart from segments from this treatise, had Hume's entire life been a lie or, at best, a compromise? *'We must look within to find the moral quality'* was presumptuous and chimerical. And how could he dare revere and entertain Rousseau? That man and his sentimentalist, sophist philosophy who once conceitedly exclaimed that 'I believe that no individual of our species was naturally more free from vanity than myself'. For a brief moment Jakob's sense of irony returned, but he neither smiled nor laughed. But the philosophy tutor could understand and even sympathise how translations of Rousseau outsold his book ten to one. Not that Levin was bitter, nor did he feel that Rousseau was in competition with Hume (for Jakob, from snobbery somewhat, did not consider Rousseau to be a philosopher in the correct sense of the term.)

Levin had always been wary of Rousseau's promotion of the romantic and egoist's passion. A bastard offspring of the nationalism and barbarism in his works was the wind which bloated the sails of barrel-chested Nazis. Such was the country's blood lust and hysteria that these sails were tempered not by the tiller of reason – the vessel had sailed blindly into a tempest and whirlpool of its own creation. But to what shores had Jakob's dispassionate temper brought him? As skilled as he believed he was with a tiller he was directionless, for no wind fed his sails. He was perpetually becalmed, a ghost ship at the mercy of the fathomless, indifferent tides. Perhaps the trick is not to reach some kind of utopian shore at all but merely to keep the weather beaten ship afloat. Jakob didn't know – but the agnostic experienced a wry sense of enlightenment when his eyes scanned over the words of another quote, from Kierkegaard, from a book the captain had also read in his youth.

'Philosophy cannot and should not give faith.'

CHAPTER TWENTY-THREE

Jorge Albetz's office was spacious and plush. A Renoir and Manet could be found amongst other lavishly framed artworks upon the walls. Fischer sat on one of two saddle-brown leather chairs which flanked a large walnut desk, rumoured to have once belonged to Talleyrand. A warm breeze wafted the subtle scent of the freshly cut flowers upon the lawyer's windowsill around the opulent chamber. Robert and his old friend from college had just completed their business and were presently working their way through a bottle of specially imported tawny port.

Robert was his lawyer's senior by but a couple of months; the pair had been each other's drinking (and whoring) companions for as long as they could both remember – indeed their friendship was partly borne from the fact that they were the only ones at college who shared the same expensive and dissolute tastes. They parted company when Robert left to travel and Jorge enrolled in law school but when they met again by accident a few years ago at a Party function it was as if nothing had changed – Jorge Albetz was still Werner to Fischer's Pechorin.

The years had been as kind to Jorge Albetz as they had been

to his friend and client. Successful without being a slave to his ambition the lawyer, a devotee of semantics and cynicism, was courted by the town's best society on a professional and social level alike. Jorge Albetz first made a name for himself as a young lawyer when he worked upon the wording and drafting of the Nuremburg Laws. Sartorial, charming, and an astute reader of both people and the times, no sooner did Jorge ingratiate himself into the Party circle than its pseudo-intellectuals ingratiated themselves to the classically educated lawyer. For a time, as with his friend Robert, the detached and amoral lawyer became fascinated with the Party and its neurotic characters on an almost clinical level. The Superfluous Men couldn't help but admire the daring and skill of the social engineering and propaganda; they were amused at the mob's hysteria and willing enslavement to the thuggish regime, or political religion. Aye, at times the tribe behaved with religious mania they surmised. Like Robert also, Jorge Albetz was a past master of turning a blind eye and deaf ear when his conscience would grumble like his stomach on witnessing atrocities and cruelty. And like his friend, his anxiety had been sublimated into conceding to women and wine, rather than pity and defiance.

The lawyer ran his palms along the sides of his head and smoothed his already slicked back ebony hair, its sheen matching that of the veneer of his polished furniture. His fingers contained a wedding band and Party ring and his nails were finely manicured. Jorge pursed his lips and exasperatingly shook his head at his friend, downing another glass of port.

"As your friend and lawyer – and I dare say speaking for your accountant – I should tell you that I am not happy about these arrangements, Robert."

"I am not doing this to make you happy Jorge," Robert replied, touched a little by his friend's concern – a commodity he was far from generous with on most occasions.

"You do know that this is well over half your estate here?"

"Well, you always say that if you can't do anything with style, don't do it at all – even build a hospital," Robert countered, amused a little by the fact that he was confounding Jorge, who only last month declared that nothing surprised him anymore.

"And how am I supposed to get the money to this Jakob Levin? Who is he? Do you not think that it is a bit too much for one man, and a Jew at that?" The Party member arched his eyebrow and gave his friend and client a suggestive look.

"I never heard you complain in the past that it was too much money for me to be in possession of. You need only carry out the instructions in that letter if something happens to me. If it proves difficult to find him after the war I suggest that you get in contact with a nurse at the hospital, Charlotte Friedrich."

"It will be more as your friend than as your counsel that I'll carry out your instructions, but nevertheless I'll carry them out. I am certainly not looking forward to the talks with the Bishop about leasing out the cathedral for the hospital. The clergy make even us lawyers look principled. But what of the devilry of the Mayor's party soon? Who are you going to accompany to the event to induce envy in us all this time?"

"I don't know. No one," Robert replied, wishing he could shed his skin of his past reputation.

"I imagine that will draw even more gasps, the renowned philanthropist and philanderer turning up alone. There must be someone you're itching to get your teeth into."

"No. Apart from me of course, Jorge, there is no one special in my life at the moment," the rake dryly remarked whilst fondly and distressingly thinking upon Charlotte and his dilemma.

"Who are you deigning to take?"

"Much to the bleating consternation of my mistress, I fear I must accompany my wife."

"I really am at a loss as to why you got married, Jorge."

"Believe me Robert, your sensible bewilderment is nothing compared to my regret. If love is blind then marriage is the eye opener," the lawyer said whilst removing another cigarette from the silver case which had been a present from Albert Speer.

*

A pensive Robert Fischer returned home and intently read over again the correspondence from his young cousin. Posted months ago, God only knew where the boy was now. From the intelligence and reports he could glean from the ministry, Robert almost wished the idealistic medical orderly was dead – rather than imagining him suffering the starvation, or cannibalism, of the Russian prison camps. He remembered the puffed-up pride and triumphalism of Edwin's early letters as he embarked and arrived in Kiev. To Stalingrad and onto Moscow was the simple plan and chant. Echoing the propaganda at the time, the young soldier had sung of the fraternity between comrades. After becoming disillusioned with the powers that be and their 'crusade', the medical student began to realise the truth – and waste. After his third Reich-glorifying letter Robert had ceased to read them – he just tossed them into a draw in his desk, unopened, whenever they arrived. Yet, feeling guilty one afternoon and receiving an anxious letter from his uncle which asked if he had heard from Edwin recently, Robert had opened and read the dozens of letters his cousin had sent him.

After a break of four months between letters, Edwin – and the tone of his correspondence – changed. He often wrote how he couldn't be sure if his letters would reach his cousin but he was still compelled to collect his thoughts, even if he was talking to himself. He spoke of the suffering and bravery of both sides, the incompetence of General Paulus, the lack of provisions and air support, the ever clamping jaws of the Russian encirclement; so too however, when talking about his 'brothers' and their camaraderie, his prose could be coloured by scenes of black humour and uncommon fellowship. Robert recalled when Edwin and his friends, sitting around eating a stew which could've barely been described as soup, had a philosophical debate about the virtue that a soldier should most prize:

"Gerhard, who proposed our evening's entertainment, was first to put his penny's worth in (quite literally we each put a penny in the pot and whoever

won the debate pocketed the bounty). *You must remember Gerhard. He is the company's best horse chef. I remember when he first served it up. Someone complained and was repulsed by the idea and said 'I'm not putting that in my stomach', to which Gerhard swiftly replied 'Why? You've had worse in your bed'. Horsemeat is now a delicacy though. Anyway, Gerhard started and argued that a soldier's foremost virtue should be fortitude, for 'the victor is he who can endure the most'. Second up in our cosy threesome was one of the quartermasters, Otto. Not having fired a shot in his life, nor tended to any wounded, Otto said with some romance and belief that courage should be prized most by the soldier and indeed is the most ubiquitous trait within our own unbeatable army. Gerhard and I but tolerate his inclusion in our company because of what he can get for us as a quartermaster, more than for what he is – an ass. Aside from his bombastic display, praising to the hilt our all-powerful Aryan war machine, he is green and blind enough to believe that not only is the Fuhrer free from blame for our calamitous position – but he also has every confidence that our Leader, who doubtless is buried in some bunker somewhere a thousand miles away, will deliver us from our 'strategic defensive position'.*

And what did I add to our Hellenic dialogue? I honestly didn't know where my answer sprung from – I certainly had not thought about such a thing before – but after the word came out of my mouth I realised that I had perhaps never spoken with such veracity or feeling in my life before.

Compassion is the virtue a soldier should value most. Not only is it precious because it seems to be the rarest commodity in war, but it blesses he that displays it and he that receives it (I must confess that I here modified my argument from Shakespeare's speech on mercy from The Merchant of Venice)..."

But how can we expect compassion from an enemy who we have not once treated humanely – except in cases of men breaking policy and committing acts of individual kindness – when we have flagrantly banished compassion from our own ranks so methodically? People might say that we are soldiers, we signed up for such conditions, but more than soldiers we are men, or increasingly boys. It used to be at the hospital that we received self-inflicted wounds to hands or legs, but nowadays we are not, or rather cannot send people back home with self-inflicted wounds to the chest and stomach. For the strangeness of my answer to the question of what should be the soldier's sovereign virtue it is compassion, more than courage and fortitude, that we deserve to be shown now, I argued. Good men are suffering and dying in ways that not even the devil's imagination could conjure it... It is just one endless, blood-curdling scream... Can a man get used to this inhumanity?

I assisted in an autopsy the other day with Dr Kohler and a pathologist, sent from army headquarters. Kohler wanted to prove beyond doubt, with scientific evidence, that which we have all known for months, that starvation, just as much the T34s and Russian blitzkrieg tactic, is laying to waste the Sixth Army. The specimen we worked on was grotesquely thin and frozen to such an extent that we had to use heaters to thaw the corpse out before we could perform the autopsy. The pathologist soon examined his chest however, snapping open his ribs with a pair of surgical shears, noting, when he came to the thoracic cavity, that there was a complete lack of subcutaneous fat. For all I have witnessed these past two years cousin, transfixed and sickened looks of disbelief still lined my face when the pathologist held up the man's heart. It was no larger than a plum.

The pathologist however, who must've had his fingers crossed when he took the Hippocratic oath, had his orders and delivered his diagnosis, 'I cannot find any valid reason why this man is dead."

The two blockheaded officers representing headquarters here nodded at the servile 'specialist'. I'm not sure whether they nodded in approval at the pathologist's performance, or his favourable judgement. Perhaps they congratulated both. Not only will the truth not get back to Central Command, but it will not even get back to Sixth Army Headquarters. It's as though the word 'starvation' has been surgically removed from our language. But why does the truth need to be reported? They are already in possession of it.

Visibly disgusted, Dr Kohler left the operating room. In hindsight his and my own hope that somehow proving our case would make a difference was blatant false hope. We might as well try to wash the blackamoor white as to think we'll survive another three months. Death, with being killed in action the most merciful release, or surrender - which could well entail a fate worse than death in the hands of our brutal enemies - are our only options..."

Robert ran his hand through his crop of hair and scratched his head again. He felt terrible for the way that he had treated his cousin's correspondence. A powerful powerless wave of sympathy heaved over him for the innocents and forgotten heroes of the Front. No longer could he glibly classify them, like Jorge had often done, as worker or soldier ants, sacrificing themselves for their Austrian pied-piper. They were men – most of them basically honest, most of them basically good; they had just been led astray like children by a seductive bully and their own ignoble instincts.

Dwelling upon his cousin's tragic fate, Fischer's thoughts inevitably turned to the awful, bloody vice which he, the town, and Germany were about to be caught in. Like those poor souls upon the Front his Scylla and Charybdis would be Hitler and Stalin – and their two transgressing, blood-thirsty packs. Jorge had reported to Robert some of the details of the meeting involving the town's mayor, General Haber, and the other wise men of the province. Heinrich Pohl, a high ranking and respected magistrate, hesitantly raised the issue and option of surrender. Showering the room with spittle, curses and propaganda, General Haber settled the argument by resolutely declaring that surrender should not even be considered an option, for "Too much German blood has been spilt."

"I don't believe I was the only one in that room, Robert, to agree with Haber in that too much German blood had been spilt. But that was the argument for surrender, not the one for nullifying the option," Jorge confessed to his friend that afternoon. "Although I dare say we were all simpatico on the issue of not bringing up the subject of surrendering the town again, especially with two devious and deviant looking Gestapo officers perched in the corner of the room. I pray they have reached their quota of executions and denouncements for the week, else Heinrich might feel the hairs upon the back on his neck bristle with the tip of a gun barrel. His young wife would not lack for consoling mourners at the funeral, however. Now there's one heavenly body worth gravitating around."

Robert didn't doubt the veracity of his drinking companion's story, nor did he have any reason to disbelieve the rumoured broadcast of Marshal Zhukov, which proclaimed, "Woe to the land of the murderers. We will get our terrible revenge for everything!"

Robert took another sip of water and thought of Charlotte, again.

This chapter closes with a brief history of Edwin Fischer. Edwin Fischer was one of the few prisoners of war of the Sixth Army who survived what can only be described as Russian death camps (these death and torture factories, every bit as dehumanising and brutal as the Reich's own Dachau and Birkenau, Edwin Fischer argued). On returning home, Germany and Germans made him feel nauseous. He felt too much shame. There were too many bad memories. He could not settle, so he took the decision to move to America and worked as a male nurse. Fischer married Felicity Lane. Initially their relationship was professional – Felicity was a *New York Times* reporter whose brief was to write an article about Russian prison camp survivors. But the pair quickly fell in love and were married. Edwin Fischer went on to become a respected historian on the subject of World War II. He was widowed in 1970 but never remarried. He passed away in 1980.

CHAPTER TWENTY-FOUR

Dirty linen was heaped in the corner waiting for the hump-backed porter to collect it. Used bandages sat waiting to be re-used. The incoherent ramblings of an amputee conversed and competed for attention with the relentless groans of a burns patient who would not make it through the night. The fetid smell of gangrene and mortality poured like smoke slowly out of the claustrophobic wards and down every passage into every cove of the hospital, including the canteen. Patient numbers were climbing as high as the damp. Infection killed as many as wounds. Veterans and raw recruits alike came in equally traumatised, their gashes running inexplicably deep. Teeth chattered like crickets, bed-wetting was too ubiquitous a problem to address and staff worked around the clock trying to put out the endless forest fire with a weakening bucket chain. Serious and fatal errors in treatment became as varied as they were commonplace. A nurse had tried to take the pulse of a patient from the Eastern Front the other day and a couple of fingers tore off in her hand from frostbite.

Charlotte sat in the canteen with a cup of black coffee that made her wince; an envelope rested on her lap and a book was open and being half read in her hand. The well-thumbed volume was an edition of Alexander Pope's poetry and she read over it again, memorizing, as if for a test, the epigram 'The Balance of Europe':

> *"Now Europe's balanced, neither side prevails;*
> *For nothing's left in either of the scales."*

Despite its poignancy – and Charlotte being amused by the opening lines of Pope's 'On the Characters of Women' – she was far too distracted and began to address again the contents of the envelope.

The young woman gazed portentously upon the invitation. Quite literally it was going to be the party to end all parties – 'everyone who was no one' was going to be there, Robert had joked. It was to be the last gathering of 'society' before their exodus. The Russians were coming, pouring down from the northeast like a glass of claret being spilt over the map. After reading over the invitation to the Mayor's party, running her fingers over the gold leaf, Charlotte unfolded and read to herself once more the note contained in the envelope.

> *"Dear Charlotte, as you may or may not know the Mayor is hosting a party tomorrow night. I know that it is quite late notice but please let me know should you be free to attend. It would just be as friends of course. If you cannot make it I will understand. Jakob said that he received a letter*

from you the other day. Please know that you are still free to call around at any time and visit him. As I am now out of the house for most of the day he has little or no company. All the information you need about the ball should be printed on the enclosed ticket. Please do get in touch, even if you cannot make it tomorrow evening. Thank you. Your friend, Robert."

To read this note one might conclude that our Captain spared all of two minutes to scribble it, but yet hours were spent in his darkened office deliberating and executing the delicate offer. The attention and sensitivity of Robert in composing the invitation was now suitably matched by the scrutiny and value Charlotte attached to it – she even examined Robert's handwriting in the word 'friends' to see if there were any telling changes inwrought within it.

After her initial shock and dissection of Robert's note Charlotte considered casually accepting the offer. Her mind then wandered and began to compose novel scenes and dialogue during the imagined ball, with the girl's literary sensibility being the ghost writer to her heart. The vignettes all ended favourably, if differently; Robert opened up to her and confessed his intention of resigning his commission; or after his simple and sincere declaration of love Charlotte cupped his face in her hands and she kissed his eyes. The scenes played out would be akin to Chekhov. Charlotte developed writer's block as to what would happen after the party however. What and where would the kiss lead to? What happened behind closed doors to the characters in these novels? Ideally she wanted to be married first, to be in love before making love. The virginal would-be authoress lacked the material to draw from to paint the undiscovered country. And Charlotte wasn't a character from a novel. A fleshy sense of worry clouded over the girl's day-dream and sucked her back into the real, prosaic world; the real world where her head was a gelding to her passions. This real world was also a cruel one for so often it proved to be contrary to people's dreams. How did she know what he really felt? How could she really trust him? And what pride and flattery she might experience from walking through the door with the officer on her arm would be soon guillotined by the jealously and sniping of the socialites at the function.

Charlotte reproached herself again for dwelling too much upon the officer. What good would it do? Her quality and quantity of work had declined as a result of the distraction of the captain. But the sensible girl could not stop thinking about him.

Since their moment together, Charlotte had been in a stupor – certainly she was critical that she often sleep-walked through her duties. The puzzle of Robert Fischer held as much possession over her as her self-possession. There were still too many pieces missing. The smallest thing, a phrase or gesture by a patient, a particular coloured tie or cut of a suit, brought the romantic figure of Robert back into focus for the young nurse. He haunted her dreams. Charlotte lived but when re-living that kiss, that pulsating moment in which she offered up herself in his firm embrace. Lost and found. She could still feel the tingle of his stubble upon the edge of her cheek; it wasn't even a particularly pleasant sensation but yet it was a sensation. But was he just a sensualist? Was he

Wickham more than Darcy? Was this invitation but an attempt at a second sortie? Instead of Raskolnikov, who Charlotte sometimes fancied she could see parallels with, was Robert ultimately a Svidrigailov? Charlotte shuddered uncomfortably and packed the comparisons back into a box immediately.

But had she not enjoyed the sensation?

It takes two people to kiss.

"A penny for them, not that I wouldn't pay more for the private thoughts of Charlotte Friedrich. Is that an invitation to the Mayor's ball? I see we're moving up in the world. I didn't know you were seeing anyone."

Stefan Numan had suffered a certain amount of anxiety, which soon mutated into jealousy, ever since Charlotte began to regularly visit the house. Just as much as Robert and Charlotte, the doctor had suffered sleepless nights of late, dwelling upon the potential couple – and coupling. His unconscious had cruelly inflicted a dream upon him in which the snake had successfully tempted his Eve, coiling himself around her limbs – with Stefan waking up in a cold sweat and the salacious impressions still branded on his waking mind. Such was Stefan's feverish curiosity to dispel or confirm his worst fears he now uncharacteristically felt emboldened to casually interrogate his unrequited love.

"I'm not." Charlotte responded defensively to the doctor's intrusive remark.

"Who is the invitation from then?" Stefan inquired whilst rudely peering over to get a better look at the card.

Charlotte was aware of the doctor's affection and intentions towards her. His increasingly frequent veiled comments regarding the captain or army officers in general were borne more from envy than from any brotherly concern. But his affection could or would never be returned. Charlotte didn't, couldn't, feel for Stefan what she felt – for *him*. Robert was like a good book that was impossible to put down – and the doctor was now proving to be an unwelcome interruption whilst reading.

"Oh, God, Charlotte, you're not considering –"

"No. I don't know. I have not made my mind up yet. I suggest that you do not make my mind up for me by attempting to forbid me from going," Charlotte said, irritated by Stefan's inquisition.

"But the man is a monster, a rake. What will people say?"

As aghast as the normally placid doctor seemed, his reaction was partly rehearsed – for before he put forward the question as to who the invitation was from, he sadly knew the answer.

"That depends on what you choose to tell them. You seem to have as much of a misconception of me as you do the captain. He is far from being the monster that some people make him out to be; whether their judgement stems from ignorance or envy I am not sure. You seem more qualified to answer that than me."

By now Charlotte was fanning the flames of her own fire, enlivened as she was with Robert Fischer-like invective. Stefan was taken aback by Charlotte's forwardness. But, as much as he had touched a nerve and he feared for the consequences of the exchange, Stefan felt it was his duty, regardless of his feelings for Charlotte, to warn the young woman of the dangers of forgetting herself in relation to the notorious officer.

I'm doing this for you.

"It'll end in tears, I'll tell you that now, Charlotte. The man puts the very devil himself to shame."

"It appears to me here, now, that Robert is twice the man you are, Stefan."

You can imagine the look upon the spurned doctor's face. As she delivered this vituperative thrust her eyes were uncommonly hardened. Her mouth half raised itself in something that might have even resembled a sneer. Charlotte knew exactly what she was saying and how much it would hurt her well-intentioned but pathetic colleague. Women can be cruel, even the nice ones. The pride and satisfied feeling that Charlotte felt at the vanquishing of the rude doctor was not an altogether unpleasant experience - though Charlotte would regret her behaviour later on, contracting an itchy sense of guilt and embarrassment when she finally encountered the doctor again. Stefan however, still obsessed with the nurse, would forgive her.

The demoralised surgeon was going to reply, "that is why it will all end in tears", but he merely timidly offered, "it's just that I'm worried about you". The picture he held in his mind, treasured like a curl of golden hair retained in a locket, of Charlotte warmly smiling at him over a beautiful child who they had just saved the life of was a world away now from the nurse's present offended and offensive glare. Stefan would conclude later that night, alone in bed, that it was the damned Captain's fault. *Fischer is deceiving her, or himself.*

After Stefan had taken his leave, bowing and shaking his heavy head as he turned his back on the stubborn and foolish nurse, Charlotte thoughtfully painted a picture in her mind's eye of a future with Stefan as compared to one with Robert. Charlotte would never have to worry about Stefan being unfaithful to her. He would be devoted to her, think himself fortunate. Life would always be seemingly contented and comfortable. But Charlotte would always consider him somewhat predictable and unromantic – and didn't Robert memorably assert that 'boredom is the root of all evil'? What would her father have thought of the two men? He wouldn't have approved of the contrary officer, but Stefan too he would've called a dullard – to his face even perhaps she granted and smiled, remembering her forthright father. Was Charlotte being mercenary, or merely human, when she considered also the glittering material life and prestige that Robert could offer her as compared to Stefan? There was no contest between the two. With Robert she could be every girl's dream, a princess, but with Stefan she was more likely to play Cinderella the housemaid to a priggish step-brother. Yet Charlotte had no desire to be every girl's dream of a princess, or at least she told herself this. But her Prince Charming was exciting and he touched the girl more deeply than any other man could. She could not help but indulge in the scenario of what a domestic life with Robert would be like. They would travel and regularly visit the theatre. They would still walk and picnic in the park. They would swap books in bed – and she would encourage Robert to write, an ambition of his that he had one afternoon surprised himself by confiding in Charlotte. The wedding would be small (they would have need of none but their own society). Their children would want for nothing - and mother and father rather than nannies and tutors would bring them up. They would be given the best educations, boys and girls – and power would be married to a sense of responsibility in their chosen careers. Even Robert's flaws could be excused, seen as attractive and ultimately curable, by the nurse's hand. Robert could even make her laugh more than Stefan could, usually a contest won by the less fancied suitor. Charlotte smiled to herself now, remembering some of Robert's comments. He described Military Intelligence as 'an oxymoron' – and a politician was 'someone who is willing to lay down another man's life for his country'.

As well as cynicism, they also shared a love of literature. He had introduced her to Turgenev, she had lent him Hawthorne's 'The Scarlet Letter'. Charlotte realised that Robert could almost make her smile, laugh and also cry at will; it was a peculiar, inspiring, unnerving revelation. As Stefan was pathetic in his would-be devotion, was she not pathetic too, and heading for a fall? As Stefan was devoted to Charlotte, was she not similarly obsessed with *him*? Civilisation is discontent. We always desire that which cannot be gratified; and if it is gratified, the desire becomes negated or but a grubby shadow of the dream. Was that why the officer had shown such an interest in her? Did he wish to obtain her because she was different – more of a challenge? She winced at such a dark thought and depraved portrait of the officer. Robert was surely intelligent enough to appreciate how lust was empty – a sin. Charlotte was not going to the topic of some lewd conversation between cigar puffing, cognac swilling, so-called gentlemen, a notch on a philanderer's bedpost. The consummation of a relationship signalled the end of the affair in some minds; once they had their wicked way they moved onto their next subject as though the act meant nothing to them. Her father and aunt had warned her about such men. And Charlotte was not and could not be that kind of girl. 'A leopard does not change his spots' Eva had warned her in relation to the infamous womaniser. So too for good measure the slightly envious and puritanical Eva reiterated how not all the stories about the captain could be but gossip, 'mud sticks for a reason.'

CHAPTER TWENTY-FIVE

The resolve of Wolfgang Nerlinger to murder his tormentor dissolved, yet the dyspeptic 'Over Man' would still take his revenge. Wolfgang planned to rob the captain. Between his fervent vow to murder the vile officer and this expedient compromise, Wolfgang had been enveloped by the trappings of vengeance. It didn't help that he proved to be his own witch doctor in pricking a doll of himself with the needles of regret and un-satiated justice; bile, like magma, stirred in the pit of his stomach and the image of the arrogant officer smugly grinning over him was indelibly carved into the old man's thoughts. If only he had acted then. Revenge is such that it will even spite the avenger; it seems to have a will of its own and can fan the flames of its own passion. One might not consider vengeance to be a seductress, or feminine even, but when its poisoned dagger sheaths itself on one's heart it can be as hard to deny as Calypso or Lamia.

During the past few weeks Wolfgang had gathered a certain amount of intelligence on his subject. Added to what he already knew or speculated upon, he talked to various sources, such as Christian, and a former manservant who Fischer had dismissed for pilfering and harassing female members of staff. He spoke to men who claimed to know the well-connected officer in the tavern. In short, Wolfgang concluded that the captain was a rich, spoiled, over-privileged playboy. Worse, a Jew lover. Apparently he was engaged for a year to a Jewess during his early twenties but his fiancée had passed away suddenly, from a lung haemorrhage, a month before his wedding. He was supposedly informed of the news whilst patronising the local brothel. Shortly after his fiancée's death, the wastrel dropped out of university and travelled around Europe for a year or so – England, France and Russia. Wolfgang was given two explanations for the dilettante's sudden departure. One story involved him assaulting a priest upon hearing the news that he had been abusing pupils in his care, including Fischer's nephew – and to avoid prosecution the guilty Fischer swiftly left the country on the advice of his family's lawyer. The other explanation, however, was that his father paid for his only son to leave the country so he could clear up a separate mess, that of getting a retarded chambermaid with child. When Fischer returned to Germany he began to win favour and influence in high circles from playing host to various German and American industrialists, investing in and promoting the interests of US companies hoping to expand their market share in Germany's growing economy. With the capital earned from pimping himself out to these American companies the self-serving entrepreneur, recognising the growth market before the war, bribed the requisite minister so as to win the contract for becoming the principle producer of buttons for the German

Army's uniforms. His wealth won him further influence and friends in the highest political and social circles – and when war broke out a commission was bestowed upon him. Rumour had it that he bribed a General so as to achieve certain tax exemptions that the rank brought with it. Along the way the profligate had been involved in numerous scandals, such as his affair with the wife of a prominent politician and the alleged shooting of a doctor who challenged him to a duel. But Fischer had always bought or wormed his way out of prosecution – and he was still feted by fellow officers and hostesses alike.

Such was the captain's standing – and connections – that it was a determinative factor, along with the embittered fascist's cowardice and fear, to alter his plan away from murdering the captain; his death would neither go un-investigated or unpunished. Aye, Wolfgang even had to be guarded in his inquiries with some of his unwitting informants. For every two people who testified to the captain being wayward and egotistical there was another who would genuinely speak well of him, citing his intelligence, sense of humour and generosity. There were also conflicting reports in regards to the Captain's relationship with his wealth – for instance he had recently let much of his household staff go at short notice, but paid them all a handsome lump sum. Furthermore Fischer was considered both ruthless and parsimonious in matters of business, but at the same time he was renowned in the town for being a patron of the arts and various other charities. The impression that the captain's wealth made on Wolfgang inspired in him the idea to rob his enemy. The idea gained even greater currency when a window of opportunity, the night of the ball, opened up – as if Wolfgang's salivating dreams regarding the money were not enough. Wolfgang further considered fortune to be on his side when he realised that the only person who would be present in the house on the night would be the snivelling Jew – and he would be incarcerated. The good national socialist would have no qualms as to murdering the source of his frustrations. Aye, revenge no longer gnawed at the liver of Wolfgang as if he was Prometheus - but rather he began to sup upon the fruits of his prospective vengeance.

Wolfgang also licked his lips at the thought of the retribution he would soon gain in relation to the gullible Christian. For all intents and purposes Christian believed that his friend was going out tonight to murder his former captain. As much as he might have wished death or injury upon the officer who at the signing of a piece of paper had made him a traitor and deserter, Christian was surprisingly indifferent to the success of Wolfgang's mission. The slovenly tenant even hoped for a moment or two that his friend would fail in his attempt and be murdered himself. Indeed Christian was far from indifferent to this outcome; not only had he grown to resent his old drinking companion but he reasoned every now and then that it was his fault that he was trapped in the unenviable state he was in. Was it not his idea to torment the Jew? He was the one who went too far. Christian considered that he could comfortably live out the rest of the conflict without Wolfgang in the short time that it would take for the Russians to arrive and liberate him. Aye, Christian could live out the rest of the war quite comfortably indeed if he found the money that he suspected Wolfgang hoarded somewhere in the apartment, like Fagan, beneath the floorboards. Such was the attractiveness of the idea of Wolfgang's demise to Christian that he imagined, in the odd idle moment (which were not infrequent), the mechanics of smothering the old man with a pillow with only one hand; or how to silence a gun shot and, without suspicion, dispose of his bloody corpse. Yet these were but ultimately fanciful notions, for Christian was as ineffectual and inebriated as ever. In the end he was also cautious in how much he wished for Wolfgang to get his just desserts, for wouldn't the apartment be immediately searched in the police investigation after any failed murder attempt?

"Are you leaving then?"

"Yes. Did I not tell you that Wolfgang Nerlinger would have his revenge, eh? I was but biding my time. If the snake has only a single venomous bite, he waits for the right moment to strike," Wolfgang declared whilst wagging his finger in the air - and then gouging out a mound of green wax from his ear with it.

Initially Wolfgang had asked his friend if he wanted to assist him. Another pair of hands, so to speak, could prove useful should there be any trouble; so too he would be able to harvest more valuables. But that was before he had decided to abandon his deserting comrade.

"You owe that zhid as much as I do," Wolfgang had issued in order to persuade the reluctant soldier a week ago, "I am going to steal so much from that Jew-loving traitor that the Mayor will be inviting me to his next party, in place of him."

Christian, partly out of trepidation but more so out of not wanting to get involved in Wolfgang's revenge, snubbed his enthusiastic comrade however.

"Only the weak do not have an appetite for revenge," Wolfgang sagely pronounced in his response.

"Then I am weak," Christian replied, openly bored by the crone's sententiousness.

"I'll give the Jew your regards nevertheless."

"If you must give him anything, give him my apologies," Christian had sulkily responded for God knows what reason. Probably he just wanted to annoy his friend.

"Ach, I cannot talk to you when you're drunk," Wolfgang said with a dismissive wave of his hand, and went out to one of his rallies (where Christian indulgently pictured the old Nazi quite literally falling off of his soapbox).

In reply to Wolfgang slamming the door, Christian, alone, sullenly murmured, "I only wish I was drunk."

"Have you got everything?" Christian now asked, still somewhat unsure that his friend was finally about to put his plan into action.

"Yes."

As the old devil made this reply he brandished his beloved Mauser and a crooked smile. His lop sided grin, revealing a set of teeth as yellow as sulphur, was brandished partly from the fact that he did indeed have everything. Also contained in the swag bag were all his papers and personal effects. Wolfgang indulged himself in the scenario that, if his venture were successful he need never return to this hole, nor share the same air as the primate again.

"Good luck."

In Christian's encouraging smile there was a conscious sense of sarcasm. Wolfgang nodded appreciatively and left, innocent of his friend's ill feeling towards him. Christian finished off in one gulp the quarter of a pint of his warm, thin beer. He loudly placed the glass back on the table and yawned-cum-roared at the same time. The torpor was only broken when the lout broke wind. He then burped. As Christian sat with a sorry look of vacancy upon his flabby, bearded pate, his belly threatening to pop the buttons on his off-white shirt, he cut a pathetic figure – more comical than sad. All that was missing was for his tongue to be drooping out of the side of his mouth like a dog, one might have fancied.

It was far from an epiphany or some moment of climax but Christian admitted a certain gloom and honesty into his thoughts. He wished that he could turn back the clock of his life; he would have studied more at school; he wouldn't have entered the army. In a moment of clarity he admitted that he was ignorant (though of precisely what he was ignorant of, or what was missing from his life, he was clearly unsure). But a pensive Christian surmised that Wolfgang was conceited and was ignorant of his ignorance – a greater crime. A simple folk song or children's story was worth a thousand of his self-glorifying pamphlets. As the old soldier held up a half empty bottle of wine, akin to Hamlet holding up Yorick's skull but not quite, Christian saw a distorted reflection of himself in the glass; the distortion of his face somehow reminded him of the Jew – and the memory of him doubled-up in agony on the floor like a baby. He looked as if he were about to sneeze, or weep. Christian was not himself though, it was the drink. He thankfully switched the radio on and the patriotic German's torpidity soon returned, dulling the pain.

*

Robert never sent off the papers ordering the soldier to be posted to the front; the disillusioned deserter was only condemned in his own mind, but yet Christian still conspired – and was conspired against – to be stranded in no man's land.

CHAPTER TWENTY-SIX

It was for the first time in a long time that the Babbel Function Hall had not been used for a Party meeting. Black, oak beams criss-crossed the ceiling and gazed down on about two hundred people – the dregs of the cream of the town's society. A teutonically polished dance-floor sat in between a large stage, with an accomplished chamber orchestra on it, and a phalanx of tables seating two hundred and fifty. The room was a cacophony of elegant music, Dionysian enthusiasm and babbling conversations.

As tastefully and stylishly as some of the ladies were dressed, Robert did not believe they redeemed the rest of the gaggle. The gaudy competed with the garish, with vulgarity the victor. Jewellery bedecked some of the women as if they were walking Christmas trees. Robert likened the fluttering nymphs at the ball to moths. Some were lissom through starvation. In the most colourful and skimpy costumes imaginable they flitted their way from one gay officer to another, climbing the ranks, to encircle the brightest rising star – laughing and smiling effusively but falsely, but winningly. He smiled to himself as he noticed a couple of women in the same lime green strapless outfit, capped off with identical hairstyles sporting matching ostrich feathers which, like rabbit's ears, stood to attention upon their heads. No doubt the two ladies of fashion had spotted each other as they strategically and mutually avoided being in the same vicinity. However, the pair were probably thinking different things; the more attractive of the two, with the svelte figure and dusky features, was doubtless fearing the sniping that would ensue for being discovered as being unoriginal and sharing the same taste as the other – older – woman who was herself religiously keeping her distance from the flagrant beauty, who put her figure and features to shame in the same outfit. Suffice to say that neither wished to invite comparisons.

The younger and comelier of the two women who shared the same outfit and fashion magazine subscription Robert had the misfortune to overhear:

"To think that we might be fortunate to see the dawning of a new millennium at the end of the century. Just imagine what the party will be like then," she enthused.

"Yes, what do you think you'll do for your millennium celebrations?" her less pretty but equally empty-headed companion replied in a girlish voice betraying her tender years.

"Something memorable, with someone half my age hopefully," she said, squealing with laughter.

Robert also observed, in a state of amusement and abhorrence, some debutantes from the Great War. The menopausal socialites, looking coldly and jealously down their aquiline noses at the shameless hussies who entertained the officers as they once did, were all dressed in embarrassingly low cut dresses revealing much, but offering little. It occurred to Robert that half of them were wearing too much make-up, the other half not enough. It is almost a precept of society nowadays that the least qualified and deserving of the role demand to be the centre of attention. They all stood together in a perfectly formed circle, no doubt conscious of the fact that if one of them dared to break ranks from the clapped-out clique, they were liable to find a verbal knife sheathed in their back.

It wasn't before long when Robert turned his splenetic humour upon the uniformed cretins littering the room. He was almost physically sickened by their poses and the glassy heat in their eyes – their vacuity was their most substantial feature, he half-jokingly posited. You would not know it from the choleric tone of his thoughts now but the severe looking Captain had entered the hall in an almost Panglossian mood – albeit no doubt a Voltairean mood was trailing not too far behind, as chaperone. The cause for which was the prospect of seeing Charlotte, although she had not replied to his letter. Yet he had faith that she would come. Such were the speeches that Robert had re-drafted and rehearsed over in his mind that he thought, for once, his words might not mock his sentiments. She was different. He was different when he was with her, better. Or he wanted to be worthy of her. She never asked anything of him except that which he needed to ask of himself. He realised how much he missed their afternoon walks in the park. For the first time since Rebecca he was happy to be just friends with a woman, which is why he wanted now to be more than just friends. He smiled, thinking how he could not remember the last time he had felt this hopeful – or fretful.

Yet these sadists and acolytes soon dragged Robert's buoyant mood back down to earth as they inspired in him a familiar strain of contempt; these descendants of roaches and bacteria, formed from retarded proteins and chimpanzee DNA, proved that man could be less than the sum of his parts. The Captain casually leaned against the bar and lightly amused himself again by happily resenting his fellow guests. Robert not only despised these buffoons because they were buffoons, but equally so his blood boiled from the fact that he envied these creatures, their capacity for self-delusion and bad faith. If ignorance was bliss then they were sipping champagne in paradise. But, underlying the officer's grating resentment and envy, an animosity nettled which was borne from the prospect that he too was manufactured from the same template and programmed with the same biological make-up. But had he not recently tried to re-write that base programme? Or were his lies and follies merely just pronounced differently? They believed in Hitler, he believed in God. What was the difference in the cosmic scheme of things, especially in the absence of a cosmic scheme to things?

Sooner rather than later, however, Robert seemed more concerned with downing another glass of watered-down cognac than keeping his head up to see if Charlotte had walked through the door. Charlotte had not responded to his note but, like any young lover, he tried to wear hope on his breast like a buttonhole.

An hour or so soon sank into the abyss and kaleidoscope some people call the past. Charlotte was still nowhere to be seen. Robert still stationed himself at the bar. Fortunately he had consumed enough cognac for the harshness of his hostility to melt away like the ice sculptor of an eagle which was perched upon a medieval banqueting table, underneath the glare of the lights. Somewhere, in the blink of an eye, with the flash of a drunkard's reflective grin, the officer swam in that mood which allowed him to laugh at his own snobbery and pride. Alcohol took its medicinal, sobering effect.

"No doubt you are amused by someone, rather than by something."

It was Julie Zidane. They had not seen each other for about five years; he had met her in Geneva, they had been lovers for about two months but then Robert was called away on business (some of his workers, peasants, "were rebellious as well as revolting," he stated at the time). Before he could return to Geneva, Julie sent him a letter informing him that she had to leave for Brussels – her aunt having been taken ill. It was perhaps as a result of this premature ending to their affair that Robert here surprised himself by how much he was pleased to see Julie again after all these years. The murmuring flames had never been doused with the cold water of familiarity and monotony. The widowed aristocrat had a lot going for her, Robert recalled. The cut of her elegant dress – a full length emerald satin gown trumpeting out at her feet that hugged her sculptured figure – reminded him how fine and smooth her neck and shoulders were. Such was the courtesan's good breeding and wit that Julie was one of the few women who could justly be a snob, like Robert. Her dry intellect and waspish sense of humour were two of the things that had attracted her to him, the priapic officer suddenly remembered. Despite always being stylishly dressed and admired for her classical features, Robert did not consider Julie to be any great beauty, although some would disagree. Her face and jaw were slender to the point of being sharp. For Robert the most pronounced feature a woman should show is her compliance, not her pointed chin. Her eyes were grey and cold, like her ex-lover's could be. Robert could also note how unnaturally un-endowed Julie was, although she now wore a black, silk wrap to keep her discreet bosom discreet – but the officer had prior (carnal) knowledge. Yet she would not have been Julie Zidane had she not an aristocratic air and haughty look; apparently she could trace her family line back to the Hapsburgs. She belonged to another century, which was partly why, even now, Robert was perhaps so coolly attracted to her.

"Miss Zidane (Robert had already covertly checked to see if there was a ring upon her finger), you are one of the last guests I would have expected to meet here – but yet one of the first people I would wish to meet. What brings you to our doomed little town?"

Robert couldn't hide the pleasure in his voice and light in his eyes at seeing Julie, or rather the womanising officer did not hide it.

"Now that I have arrived (Julie here arched her thin auburn eyebrow and condescendingly looked around her) I am asking myself that very same question."

Julie smilingly looked the handsome officer up and down, surveying her ex-lover with eyes that purposely flickered with play and desire. A wanton smile also purred upon her scarlet lips from remembering one of the last times that she had seen her old flame. It was in the austere atmosphere of Zurich's Museum of Fine Art. They freed themselves from the tourist's orientation and had made love to each other with appetite and harmony in the curator's office. Such was their passionate abandon though that Robert tore Julie's blouse in the process. With the weather that June being as heated as their passion she hadn't a coat to cover herself up. Ever Julie's mercurial hero though, Robert crept into the museum's cloakroom and stole a jacket. Such was the thrill and romance of the episode that the Chanel coat too was nearly rendered sleeveless as they made love, with a depravity and ecstasy that the convent educated Julie had not known before (but afterwards practised) back in the hotel room.

"I know, I have put on weight. Rather than being overweight however, I like to think of myself as being twice the man I used to be."

"And are you twice as wealthy? Five years ago you considered yourself as wealthy as sin."

Julie couldn't tell whether the officer was being sarcastic or not, but he here replied, "Wealth, as well as sin, cannot buy you happiness."

"But wealth can buy you a Mercedes. Those who say that money cannot buy you happiness just do not know the right stores in which to shop. But how unlike Robert Fischer to speak of happiness," the once mistress to a French cabinet minister, who shall remain nameless, remarked whilst playing with the pearls around her marble neck. Julie remembered how Robert had once declared how beautiful her neck and shoulders were and the arousing sensation came back to her the way he would shower them with kisses and make her sigh.

Robert was going to reply that how like Julie Zidane to talk about money but the realisation that he did not want to deride her came hand in hand with his desire to sleep with her.

"Talking of money, here comes my brother and your General Haber. It seems that you are not the only one who is as wealthy as sin Robert, my brother is now negotiating a contract for the General to move his account to our Swiss bank."

Robert now knew exactly why Julie was here. By the way the General came over and leered at Julie, with Julie reciprocating his obtuse advances, he realised that she was here as a sweetener. The war had hit the family finances. Julie had become a whore, her insipid younger brother her pimp. The General may not have been the most elderly suitor that Julie had ever had, but love would have to be blind – she would no doubt just close her eyes in her bond with the gross client, Robert thought to himself.

"Here she is, General," a suave Gustav remarked, raising his arm to his sister as if she were an object on display at a gallery. An apt description of Julie's brother would be to say that he was nondescript; he was the kind of swell who would jump into a canal twice as fast to save a drowning child, should a beautiful woman be there to witness it. Robert had thought him an odious toady five years ago – and time had not modified Gustav's character or the misanthrope's opinion of him.

"I would have hoped General, that I stood out for you."

The look upon the General's puffy face betrayed his confusion at whether he thought the sophisticated lady was teasing or reproving him. In such situations though even stout men like Lars Haber can become inspired.

"I am so blinded by your beauty madam, that my eyes are not what they were."

The picture upon the General's face was one of immense self-satisfaction, believing he had composed a compliment worthy of the lady's set, one which was worthy of Fischer even. Julie, an expert in such things, was mercurial enough to turn her look of pleasure, from amusement, to that of the pleasure of being flattered. Robert, less subtly, concealed the amusement in his countenance by expediently turning his back upon the General's unseemly courtship - and ordering another drink.

"Oh please General, you will make me blush. You say the sweetest, most gorgeous things."

Julie endearingly, amorously gazed up at the General when she expressed this. A woman's coquetry has the ability – even if we know it to be insincere – to make us believe that we reside at the centre of her universe.

The detached look on the Robert's face expressed his mood. Yet the distant officer was, at best, but half a world away. Mediocrity and falsity were all around him, overpowering him like a drab's cheap perfume. His contributions to the routine conversation involved mechanically parroting his audience's prejudices and views. Such was Robert's mood that one could have imagined him being Tolstoy's Nekhyludov from "Resurrection" repeating to himself, in the company of similar good people, 'Disgusting and disgraceful, disgusting and disgraceful' (indeed, one could have even considered Robert Fischer as being akin to a mature Tolstoy). So too might the romantic philosopher have been in agreement with the novelist's character Nekhyludov in considering Man to be a compound of an animal and spiritual self. Although in appearance the lavish ball seemed both civilised and cultured, Robert would have hesitated not in asserting that it was further proof that man was in possession of an animal self, or rather that his animal self was in possession of him. Hormones were worn in the eyes like the paste upon the ladies' ears. Primal desires of lust, displays of power, territory marking and mating rituals – some as simple as merely sniffing around the tail of a creature even – were as frugal and bland as the food. 'Error has transformed animals into men; is truth perhaps capable of changing man back into an animal?' – Nietzsche. He needed some air.

Fearing that Robert might turn his back on their civil foursome and wander off, Julie searched for any opportunity to extract the captain from his mood and involve him in the conversation. Much to her relief Julie and Robert had a chance to pick up their discussion whilst the awful General and her brother went to get some drinks after giving up on the waitresses – who were downing the drinks they were supposed to be serving and bouncing up and down upon sweaty, carousing knees.

"So, in spite of your wealth rather than because of it, surely you are not telling me that Robert Fischer, our German Onegin, is happy?"

"I am happier, if that is any sort of confession," Robert replied, partially reanimated from realising that the general and his pet would be absent for a time.

"Even after all these years I still cannot tell whether you are being serious or not."

"If I cannot tell whether I am being serious or not, do not worry too much that you cannot either – even though you do possess the philosopher's stone of a woman's intuition," the ironist said with a playful twinkle in his eye.

Unfortunately, shattering their increasingly flirtatious exchanges, the general and Gustav returned, their unwelcome swiftness being a result of the general commandeering a tray of drinks from a couple of his junior officers.

Julie's intention behind asking the question to the general first was that of using it as a prompt to then ask the other officer in their small circle.

"Tell me General, what do you plan to do after the war? No doubt the army will be dismantled."

Should those defeatist words have emanated from one of his officers, then Robert had little doubt that the General would have bellowed indignantly at them – perhaps even received the back of his hand across their face to accompany the torrent of abuse. Robert had seen the blustering General lose his temper in such a fashion before. However, his appearance was one of mortified shock; the lady received an ugly look of scorn at her demoralising and impudent question. Although Robert believed Julie capable of such spiteful artifice, it seemed that her comment was innocent. After all was the general not now planning to transfer his finances to Switzerland in anticipation of defeat?

The general's blood pressure rose, as did the colour in his cheeks. Robert wisely chose to be amused by the general, who would now have to decide between keeping his dignity and Nazism intact, or becoming disagreeable to his lady in waiting. Before the captain could be entertained by Lars Haber some more though, he was interrupted by a dutiful adjutant and Robert was starved of what would have been a delicious response for one reason or another.

"I am sorry General, but you have an urgent phone call."

"If you will excuse me gentlemen, Miss Zidane."

As the rotund General rose from his civil bow, Robert could not fail to notice his jacket stretch across his back and shoulders, fit for bursting, and his spare chin wobble like a plate of tripe. Robert had finally found his motivation to diet. That they shared the same uniform – that was all they would have in common. Should Charlotte have given the word also, he had vowed that they wouldn't even share that dishonour.

"My sister and I will await your return, General," Gustav replied with a slightly lower bow.

"Yes, do not be so naughty as to not see us again before you leave, General."

"I have no doubt at all, Miss Zidane, that we will see each other again."

Lars Haber glared at Julie lasciviously, all but licking his rubbery lips. The regal lady's stomach turned and she nearly reddened with shame for being in Robert's presence – but the experienced woman duly accepted the General's drooling attention, or intention. The 'lecherous hippo', as Julie later called him, then looked at his Captain and smugly raised his eyebrows, believing he was impressing the arch-seducer with his catch. Robert gave the general an appreciative nod but grinningly thought to himself how it was Lars who was hooked upon her line and bait.

Not twenty seconds after the general had left to answer his call, Gustav became agitated, not knowing what to do with himself apart from wipe his clammy palms upon his trousers. He had watched with care, even standing on tiptoes to do so, as the general bustled his way through the crowd. The banker was averse to letting his would-be client out of his sight. The general's signature held his future in its hands. No sooner had he disappeared when the fear rose up in Gustav's anxious mind that Haber might not return, or that he would bump into some other lady friend; having spent so much time in the company of his sister he was qualified to depreciate her value. The same age as Robert, Julie wasn't getting any younger.

"I am sorry Captain, but you must excuse us now."

"Why, where are you going?" Julie curtly remarked, looking askance at her brother.

The exaggerated hardening of his eyes and pursing of his lips acted as Gustav's blunt rebuke to his sister. Not just because of her brother's authority over her, Julie had to comply. She had to do this for herself, as well as for the family's finances.

"There is someone I would like you to meet, Julie."

In reality Gustav wanted to swiftly usher his sister off so that they would be the first to encounter the general when he returned. She flashed a milk-curdling glance at her brother but then turned to Robert with serenity and allure adorning her face. She saw her brother look away to the door where the boorish General had disappeared into and stole the opportunity to sensually whisper into her ex-lover's ear.

"I am staying in the Metternich Hotel. My room is 35b, I shall leave a note and key for you at reception."

And with this Julie ever so softly kissed and sucked upon the officer's ear lobe. After absorbing this delightful and erotic sensation, Robert made a mental note to add it to his own catalogue of seduction techniques. As Gustav led his sister off by the wrist, she darted back a sly and coquettish glance that was unbecoming to her age but arresting nevertheless; but then again the endorphins which were now being released into the German officer's blood stream meant that Julie could do no wrong.

He finally saw her. Robert perhaps recalled the heavenly image at least once every day for the rest of his life. There is a kind of beauty which can burn, as well as soothe.

Charlotte didn't mean to be so fashionably late, but she'd had to stay later than expected at the hospital. Added to this she took a suitably lady-like time in getting ready, accompanied by the background music of her cousin Eva's advice to be both wary of the captain yet also to make sure that she had a relaxed and enjoyable evening at the 'fancy' ball.

The light danced melodically and shone in and off her tightly bound, pinned up blonde hair. A couple of ringlets however still lightly hung down, framing her face. Her diamond earrings, given to her by her aunt who happily spoiled her niece whenever she could, glistened like tears. Still Charlotte wore around her supple neck the simple silver cross, once her mother's. She veritably sparkled as the graceful twenty-one year old twisted her head this way and that, ignoring various colourful sights and sounds for the trivialities that they were, searching for her Captain.

Forget Julie, which Robert easily and conveniently did, Charlotte was the beautiful figure who belonged to another century – and world. She was wearing a rustling silk ball gown of claret and blue. The elegant garment flattered, rather than cheaply revealed, a feminine figure. Unlike the various clumps of pinched faces and mannequins decorating the hall, Charlotte wore a tasteful and subtle amount of perfume and make-up; ladies, please, make-up should be a compliment to beauty, not a substitute for it - Robert had wanted to exclaim out loud earlier.

It was like someone taking Aeolus' bag of winds off his head. Robert both regained and lost possession of himself at the sight of her.

Charlotte shone with unassuming and undeniable beauty, illuminating the very air which surrounded her. She justly turned more heads than one might have expected. How much we can put it down to the drink I do not know, but Robert's usually reserved heart began to swell to the point where it could have ended up in his mouth. She was all the more striking for looking a little lost and out of place, he thought.

She spotted him, carefully making his way through the crowd. He looked pleased to see her, yet also a little drained. A relieved and radiant smile lifted Charlotte's and then the officer's features. Should you have sliced the intimidating Captain in two now you would have found the word 'Charlotte' verily written through him as though Robert were a stick of seaside rock. The officer nervously stood before her, somewhat stupefied as well; at one moment he could not take his eyes off the graceful woman for fear that she might disappear for the miracle that she was. The love-struck seducer blinked repeatedly in astonishment at Charlotte's transformation, transfiguration. But then he found he couldn't quite meet her eyes, intimidated as he was by the girl's unaffected beauty and goodness.

Charlotte realised she looked pretty – false modesty is as unappealing as unwarranted egoism – but yet how could any girl's confidence not fail to flower upon witnessing the impression she made on her would-be suitor? Was he lost for words? Love, not lust, was written in his warm expression. Charlotte lightly blushed in both pride and shame – and her heart was married to hope.

"I'm sorry for being so late."

"Trust me, you've been worth the wait. You look lovely, Charlotte." Robert was about to add that he missed her, but desisted.

He smiled again, partly to reassure her that everything was fine

- and partly because he was happy. He too would not bring up their last encounter. He just wanted to be her friend. The role of seducer was shallow and destructive, compared to what Robert now felt for the remarkable young woman.

"I am sure I have not been missed. You have been in the company of our town's best society," Charlotte slyly replied with a telling expression on her face that she had perhaps learned from observing the satirical officer. Robert appreciated the joke and similarly, endearingly, smiled in sympathy.

"'Society is now one polished horde, formed of two mighty tribes, the Bores and the Bored.' Byron."

Charlotte was impressed again by Robert's flawless English and the wit of the just epigram; she couldn't suppress grinning, though she coyly placed her hand over her mouth to conceal her pleasure at enjoying the scornful vein of thought so much.

"Would you like to sit down? You must have been on your feet all day," the officer considerately remarked.

"Thank you."

With guests criss-crossing in front of the couple as they walked towards a free table, one could not make out whether Charlotte offered Robert her hand or whether the gentleman clasped the lady's gloved palm – but Robert now lovingly, as if they were sweethearts, led his partner through the preening and uncouth throng to find some privacy and a place where they could hear each other speak. The captain was careful to not exhale over Charlotte's silken shoulder as he politely pushed her chair in for her, so as to prevent the nurse from smelling the alcohol on his breath. I should've stuck to drinking the odourless vodka Robert briefly told himself, intoxicated in quite a different way to that of how he had been earlier on in the evening.

Although appearing a paragon of grace and style Charlotte was giddy with anxiety and the thrill of first love. Her mood lightened and soared. She was flattered to distraction to think that out of all these stunningly glamorous women with their aristocratic airs and expensive dresses, Robert had chosen her. A waltz by Strauss stirred in the background, perfuming the air. Charlotte was at heart a sensible girl but she was still but a girl; her biology, as well as her bookish soul, was nubile. But she was just his friend she reminded herself, as if the young woman served as her own chaperone. Expect nothing to come from this Charlotte, therefore you will not be disappointed – she had issued to herself before the mirror whilst getting dressed. She fancied she sounded like Jakob in such a mode. How often Charlotte had attempted to analyse the officer in the past, telling herself that only she understood him, but her unloosening heart now yearned, pined, to read her officer's true feelings and intentions – if he had any. She still knew so little about him. She yearned with the romance and anxiety of a dozen sleepless nights to know if Robert had read her feelings. Did he think of her in the way in which she wished, needed to be thought of – whatever that was? Did he love her? Would he ask her to dance?

The officer's breathing became a tad heavier; his brow also shone with a glaze of perspiration in the mellow candlelight. Robert looked as if he were about to confess his sins, or declare his love to this unpretentious, spirited and witty girl who had helped save him without her even knowing. She never lied or played games with him. She made him feel young, renewed, whenever he was in her company. They both glanced at Robert's hand as it nervously fingered the smooth rim of an empty sherry glass.

"I'm sorry, would you like a drink?"

"A white wine please. Would you like me to help you?"

"No, I'll be fine. You take care of so many people during the day, Charlotte. You must now allow me to take care of you."

A girl no older than twenty dressed up in some form of a proto-catsuit rubbed up against a happy looking Robert at the bar and flashed her sugar-white teeth invitingly at him.

"Leave me alone," he said either wearily or threateningly. She tutted, petulantly tossed her strawberry blonde hair and took her leave to rub up against a reveller more susceptible to her charms. Robert lovingly stared at Charlotte. She was helping one of the waitresses clear the adjoining table. He hadn't felt this good, sure, about someone since Rebecca. He was all the more struck by how strongly Charlotte reminded him of his fiancée, for the fact that he hadn't thought about it before. He still often referred to Rebecca as *'her'* or *'she'* in his thoughts – for even now his heart and conscience quivered at best uncomfortably, at worst tortuously, at the mention of her name. How long had it been, ten, twelve years? *Some wounds just don't or can't heal.*

On the evening that he promised himself and a fair weather God that he would finally vanquish his adolescent ways – discharging any vestige of enthusiasm he still retained for the bachelor life in one last orgy of pleasure – the girl who he loved dearly, who had inspired in the nihilist a sense of abnegation and a belief in fidelity, lay in her bedroom – the life coldly ebbing away from her golden shores as fluid flooded her lungs. She died before Robert could see her. The memory of when he heard the news, the morning after in the brothel, was branded in his conscious indelibly, if only for its potent fusion of the comic and tragic that the scene was married to. His would-be brother-in-law found the groom, a jingling coxcomb on his head, sleeping and momentarily sticking onto the pillows of a high-class drab's champagne-drenched cleavage. He never got the chance to say goodbye, or sorry, to her.

As a young woman will sometimes religiously blame herself for miscarrying her child, believing some force to be punishing her for past sins, or it being a sign that she is not fit and ready to be a mother, Robert put himself through the fires of hell, finally being reborn as cold as ice, after Rebecca's death. All had been a mournful interim 'twixt then and now. Robert had promised himself a decade or so ago that he would not be scratched by Cupid's, or any other god's, arrows again; poetry was transplanted with philosophy and such was the seducer's determination to bury his heart that, should he have reared his ruddy face, the fatalist would have marched up to Cupid, confiscated his biological weapons, and snapped them all over his knee.

Robert briefly dwelled on the two women's mutual and contrasting virtues. They shared the same caring instinct, generosity of spirit and sense of duty - but Robert still believed he admired them individually. He believed that he wasn't in love with Charlotte under the conceit that if he treated Charlotte right, then he would somehow be absolved of his past sins in relation to Rebecca.

'Marry her or do not marry at all' the former philosophy student, quoting Kierkegaard, churned over in his mind. The wish that he could remain unseen as Anna Bremer and her blockhead suitor moved towards him prickled his being. The old sow, a former golden calf, and prize bull, were fit for each other Robert judged. Fortunately he shuffled into position and was able to conceal himself behind an over-zealous perm, replete with what looked like coloured eggs entangled in the bird's nest. As impatient as Robert was to get his drinks he was strangely engrossed in the scene, attracted but more so repulsed by the spectacle surrounding him – the yammering and fatuous charade. He had outgrown it all, shed his skin. He couldn't help but couple their behaviour to pigs around a trough. Perhaps it was because and not in spite of the atrocities outside these four walls that people seemed oblivious to it all. Only such an opulent, glamorous sphere, crystal and pristine like a scene from a snow shaker, could allow one to escape the absurdities and malevolence of the events beyond the Babbel Function Hall. How Robert desired, demanded, to pick up the snow shaker and violently, almost in a strangle hold, wake it up; as a substitute for artificial snow Robert pictured that sweaty, dirty tears might rain down on the party, along with hailstones of blood and ordure. He darkly imagined that, as buried as they were underground and in their gay thoughts, the dead might rise up – and that not even their anthemic music could wash away the stains that the charred corpses would make upon their silk gowns and dowdy minds. Was his idea of marriage, as equally romantic as ethically conceived, merely just another kind of snow shaker he suddenly thought?

The drawn out notes and strains of the string music echoed, or even perhaps partly caused, Robert Fischer's melancholy air as he gazed at Charlotte. If only he did not find the radiant girl so beautiful then perhaps he would not love her so much, or was it that because he loved her so much that he found her so beautiful?

Marry her or do not marry at all.

In the same way that Robert imagined that he had made a commitment towards God, could he similarly dedicate his life to Charlotte? Can one do both? Should he forsake the angelic girl who he had spent half of his life searching for? Was he deluding himself, or were his doubts the delusions? But who did he know who was happily married? And happiness was not meant for Robert - but he would do everything in his power not to make Charlotte unhappy. He did not deserve her, nor did she deserve him, he argued. He thought to himself that the only fate he did justly deserve was the penance of a life without Charlotte.

Robert transformed himself into a widower without even marrying. He had loved and lost before; maybe it is better to have never loved at all than to have loved and lost. Perhaps he was anchored down by a loss of liberty, fearful of a defining commitment. Did he ultimately feel guilty, being unfaithful to Rebecca? A part of him believed they would meet again. The comfortable bachelor was also worried in that he believed he was incapable of the routines, sacrifices and histrionics involved in playing the role of husband. Robert was all too conscious of the daily grind and tit-for-tat exchanges of married life – and how often had domesticity been akin to a lobotomy on past acquaintances? Even with the best will in the world he was just not designed to be a devoted husband and father – that which he most desired to be. A terminal depression loomed over Robert like some God-sent aegis at the thought that someday he might grow tired of Charlotte and be unfaithful to her. *Whilst the spirit is willing, the flesh is weak.* The Charlotte of today might also not prove to be the Charlotte of tomorrow. She, even more so than him, could change. There was also the age gap to consider. Love, however true and magical, cannot sustain a marriage alone. The hopes and rewards of scaling Mount Olympus are eclipsed and annulled by the dreadful prospect that the Gods might not be at home. If he did not leap then he would not fall. A thousand doubts and reasons coldly rained down upon him – as love's fountain gushed up from his heart, sprouting wings and heavenly chords. The half inebriated officer again recited, "Marry her or do not marry at all". God only knows why a desperately lonely Robert did not marry Charlotte. Happy endings are meant for characters in novels, not real people.

A peculiar, though not wholly unfamiliar numb and tingling sensation worked its way up and down Robert Fischer's left arm again. He had been leaning upon the side of the bar for the larger part of the evening. He finally received his drinks.

As much as Charlotte would soon be the condemned woman, Robert approached the girl looking like a condemned man. Even possessed by this morbid mood of conceit and masochism, Robert still found it doubly difficult to inspire in himself the necessary words and malignancy that were needed to do what – he painfully and nobly considered – was the right thing to do, by Charlotte and himself. The loveless amorist had ploughed his way through numerous affairs before which had ended abruptly, nastily, with climax and anti-climax alike – but the seducer had lost his appetite for such scenes. Charlotte was different. He tried to casually walk over to his Regina Olsen (the spurned fiancé of Soren Kierkegaard) with a glass of wine and a glass of water in his hands but the sensitive girl could sense an unnaturalness in her companion. Charlotte could see it in his eyes. He now considered that look of dark desire to be almost ridiculous but nevertheless Fischer mimicked his former self. Arrogantly – and all but callously, as if he were enacting some business transaction – the officer altered his tone.

"We should finish these quickly. I have reserved us a suite at the Bismarck and I do not want to keep my driver waiting. I promised him the evening off." Robert nearly choked on the words. Tears moistened his eyes but fell not – else they would ruin everything.

Romance-less trollops might have appreciated our officer's manly candour, if for no other reason than for the immediacy of his approach. But our modest heroine was understandably devastated. She looked at him with distress and incomprehension, as if the devil himself stood before her; her eyes lost their verve, as if put out by a blunt instrument. Charlotte's complexion turned corral-white as the blood rushed to her heart in the shock. By the end of the episode though her face twice blazed red with embarrassment and indignation. The highly-strung unstrung. Charlotte smiled nervously, hoping that it was all some kind of joke. The officer however forced himself to remain as lusty-eyed as a savage.

"Please do not play coy now. You know that this is what it's all been about. If not for you, it has been for me, Charlotte."

"How can you be so heartless? No, this is not you. Or everyone was right. They warned me. You're a monster."

"And I suppose you're conceited enough to think yourself an angel and that I do not deserve you?" the officer drolly retorted, inwardly suffering – dying.

The innocent woman's expression screwed itself up and her hand raised itself to her face as if she were about to break down. Charlotte pitifully glanced up at Robert in one last attempt to save the situation, to allow the wilful Captain to rescue himself from his condemnation. The moment, pause, would remain with Robert and Charlotte for the rest of the lives. How many times did they both play out alternative outcomes to the exchange? But Robert remained heroically ignoble.

He wished that she could have slapped him around the face, as others had done so in the past, but the nurse was too traumatised – and her character not melodramatic enough – to carry out such an act. Scurrying upon the tips of her toes as if she were a ballerina, the queasy girl covered her contorted face in her hands and fled from the party. As Charlotte broke down Robert Fischer's heart too cracked; should he not have wallowed in a state of shock and been conscious of making a scene – and holding drinks in both hands – the emotional man might have tearfully chased after Charlotte and confessed the truth, if indeed he could cage that particular animal. His thoughts swirled however and his heart sank as the excruciatingly solitary officer impotently watched the nurse being written out of his life. That it seemed for the best, from some lofty point of view, was a phrase and sentiment that would provide little comfort to the officer.

This chapter ends with the not altogether tragic herstory of Charlotte Friedrich. As her morish and romantic feelings for the Captain had mainly been a private affair Charlotte was similarly determined to conceal her heartbreak from the world. She couldn't express her state of being, nor fully comprehend what had happened, anyway; nor could she stomach people like Stefan and Eva spouting I told you so or vilifying Robert for the wrong reasons when they didn't know him. With her eyes puffy and being still in turmoil Charlotte decided, wisely or not, to walk home in order to collect her thoughts and recover her composure. The young debutante cut a surreal figure tramping halfway across town towards home. What strange and ogling looks the hysterical woman received however were ignored or unseen as Charlotte's head was bowed, deep in chaotic and abject reflection. Both her aunt and cousin knew something was amiss as soon as they saw her, but full knowing how obdurate

Charlotte could be they decided not to press the issue that night. The maudlin girl's family were soon more concerned by the fever that Charlotte fell into the morning after. At first it was but a chill, brought on from her uncovered chest when traversing home, but the ague soon mutated into an obscure strain of pyrexia. She slept sporadically, sometimes mumbling to herself from a dream or nightmare, and woke to a sweat-soaked bed. At once she was hot and then her teeth would chatter from the cold. But still the weakened nurse had to be restrained by her aunt to keep her from her duties at the hospital. In company she would grow irritable, asking just to be left alone; as soon as the fragile and sometimes delirious girl was left to her own devices though her temperature would flare up again, dwelling on the incubus of *him*. If Charlotte could have convinced herself that he was whole-heartedly the sinner and sensualist that he seemed then maybe she would've recovered from the trauma more swiftly and cleanly. Charlotte's secret desire to see the officer again, to give him a second chance and tell him that she could forgive him, was only matched by her vow that she wouldn't try to renew their friendship – if indeed there was anything to renew after the way he had treated her. As a coda to her fever and nervous depression she was troubled by the scenario that she might not see Jakob again. The nurse wrote to a letter to her former tutor however, delivered by her aunt's maid who she made swear to secrecy (she also imparted to the maid that she was on no account to give the letter to the master of the house). Charlotte informed Jakob that she was sorry for not being able to visit him but she was busy at the hospital – and would be busy for the foreseeable future.

Within a year however the war ended and Charlotte betrayed little or no trace of the delirium and resentment which had debilitated her so. I suppose you could say her relationship with the predatory officer made Charlotte a little colder and more cynical but those traits would have come with age anyway, wouldn't they? Physically Charlotte may have also been seen to change; her eyes lost their expressive lustre and seemed for some reason to have sunk back into her head; Charlotte also cut her golden locks off in order to change her appearance and look more mature when she gained a promotion. When she was happily reconciled with her father he barely recognised his little girl on the train platform. Within the year the nurse was engaged to the deputy chief surgeon at the hospital, Stefan Numan. The love between them was sparked and fuelled from the fact that the doctor owned enough good feeling for the both of them. Stefan worshipped her – which Charlotte realised and often played on to get her way. She wouldn't sleep with him until they were married. Stefan knew he had been second-choice, but at the same time considered that he had still won a victory. As much as she might have been in a position to, Charlotte could not bring herself to hurt and exploit Stefan that much. She was too kind and had herself been too deeply hurt for that to happen. It is not out of the question that the young woman married Stefan to finally exorcise her grief regarding the haunting officer – although marrying someone like Stefan could have also be interpreted as an active act of spite against someone like the egotistical Captain. It may also be said that Charlotte married the dutiful doctor out of a belief that motherhood was somehow an answer to something – that it would fill the hole left behind by all the dreams she had burned upon a funeral pyre for him. Like but yet unlike the tragic ending of Dido and Aeneas, Charlotte once conceitedly fancied.

But the marriage was more than one of just convenience. There were few moments of classic storybook romance or movie passion to their marriage but, as second best and uncultured as he was, Stefan was a good husband. He was attentive, faithful and generous. They moved to England and a picturesque old cottage on the outskirts of Dorset – which was falsely rumoured to be the love nest of a young Thomas Hardy – after Stefan retired. It had always been of dream of Charlotte's to live in England. Perhaps Charlotte's love was partly borne from the guilt and gratitude which arrested the introverted woman at not loving him enough, or loving him merely as their children's father (the couple had three children, Karl, Jakob and Maria) – but nevertheless Charlotte grew to love and respect Stefan. As unfulfilled, mournful and introspective as she was, all in all Charlotte Numan led a not altogether unhappy or unlived life.

CHAPTER TWENTY-SEVEN

The guests left two by two. Constantine Baptes, an old flame of Robert's, happily observed her former lover alone at the close of the evening and attempted to rekindle their unremarkable affair. But a saturnine Robert was not in the mood. He didn't even look at the opera singer whilst he spurned her.

"Are you not even going to speak to me?" the demure woman said, attractively standing before him in an imitation Chanel gown, her painted face coquettishly askew.

"Only to bid you goodbye and goodnight," the officer replied, tired.

"You've changed," the social lioness then sulkily emitted, upset that the red-blooded man was unresponsive to her mating signals. He had always frustrated her. She could never predict or fathom his moods, or understand why he called an abrupt end to their relationship. He had used her. She always liked to be the one to end the affair. Why didn't she satisfy him?

"I wish I could say the same about you," Robert answered, inebriated.

"You've not changed at all. Why won't you even look at me,

Robert? Do you hate me that much?" Constantine Baptes exclaimed, again dramatically altering her tone – exhibiting now self-pity. If she kept talking to him sooner or later the womaniser would look up at her and her charms would capture his aspect. Did not her looks win over audiences before she even opened her mouth when performing?

"I'm beginning to. Please, let me be," Robert said, almost despairingly.

"What's wrong? Why do you get like this, Robert? Is there anything I can do?"

"Yes, take your leave. Please, I don't wish to be rude, but if you want there to be anything between us, let it remain distance."

In the end, after recovering from the snub and arguing that she was better off without the egotistical officer, Constantine paired up with what was left on offer – a somewhat rowdy young buck, the son of a senior Party official, who would prove to be memorably forgettable by the end of the week, or night even.

The wind ululated down the alley of the building's back entrance. Intent on avoiding the congregation of revellers and maenads outside the main doors – and being unable to hire one in a line of cabs parked in front as a consequence – Robert made his own way home. He was more than content to walk, hoping that the bracing air might clear his head a little. A stygian darkness swallowed up any number of stars; inky, fungal clouds conspired to swab out the moon, which faith alone could convince one that she was still there. The firmament, mottled as if suffering from a skin disease, promised but delivered not a cleansing rain. The isolated pilgrim felt as leaden as the urban weather.

Shallow, depraved and lively were the thoughts which itched and canvassed for Fischer's attention. His pride fell on stony ground however in trying to convince the former Byronic figure that he had just created a masterpiece in self-destruction and supra-morality. Flattery and congratulations were offered, but Robert was too listless to accept. All that was left now, this voice whispered into his ear, to transcend morality and desecrate all the fictions and normality that Charlotte represented, was to turn off into Kohler Street and wait for Julie in the lobby of the Metternich Hotel. This distinct and familiar voice, the disparate man genuinely tried to dismiss but yet, like a fly around one's head, it did not completely go away and he could always hear its faint buzzing sound. This nagging voice teased the would-be Christian in regards to the irony that one of the noblest acts he had ever performed in his life would also cause a mountain of suffering. Perhaps more from the fact that he wished for this voice to just retreat – more than from its temptations – Robert allowed himself the thought of re-treading his steps and paying a visit to Julie and her suite.

*

Wolfgang could smell his own musty odour on his moth-eaten overcoat, but the garment owned the virtue of being as black as a jackdaw's breast and thus, aided by this God-sent gloomy night and keeping to the shadows, he could come and go as he pleased.

Presently however the would-be villain conspicuously stood beneath the lamppost opposite the family home of Dr Abraham Solomon. Such was his bony forehead, his bushy eyebrows and sunken pupils, Wolfgang Nerlinger was a cinematographer's dream as he stood, cadaverous-eyed, policeman-like, in the dead of the funereal night.

Wolfgang consciously allowed his revenge and racism to goad, dare and bully him into crossing the road. *It is now or never.* What was he, a man or a mouse? Jakob was awake and working in Robert's study but, as the room resided at the back of the house, Wolfgang came to the conclusion that there was nobody at home – only the Jew in the cellar, waiting to meet his fate. Wolfgang was also confident of the captain's absence as Christian had informed him that, on occasions such as the Mayor's ball, he never brought his society harlot home for the night; the captain always chose to take his whores to a flash hotel.

Should anyone have witnessed Wolfgang limping across the street, doing his best to look unassuming, no doubt they would have found him a source of mild suspicion. But, as predictable and contemptible as you might think the man was, one shouldn't underestimate him. Hitler too could have been criticised as being predictable and contemptible, but as monstrous and powerful as he became he spent the majority of his career being underestimated. Propaganda and fortune are influential, but apathy and ignorance also place such leaders on the throne – and keep them there.

Fortune smiled on the opportunist as he discovered one of the ground floor windows unlocked. Breathing heavily, almost wheezing, Wolfgang removed a folded up black bag from his holdall. He figured he could leave his belongings by the window and collect them on his way out. All the old man took with him into the house was the swag bag and his lovingly oiled pistol. Agile and reasonably fit for his age, Wolfgang hurriedly slipped through the window like a fox between the fencing of a chicken coop.

Jakob's insomnia had become his bedfellow. Masochistic regret regarding his actions (and inaction) towards both Sara and himself turned his mattress into a bed of nails. To counter claustrophobic sleepless nights Levin immersed himself in his work until he was forced into slumber by pure exhaustion. He reasoned that the demands of his body to rest could out will his mind's desire to undergo the wire jacket and death of a thousand cuts – exhuming macabre and happy memories. Jakob's workload also increased, doubled, as a result of his project to begin to translate for personal, academic reasons again. Borrowing the captain's copy, Jakob started to translate into English the short stories of Franz Kafka. As well as the captain's library Levin began to use the officer's study – now that Robert seldom occupied it. Indeed, Jakob could not fail to notice how little time the captain spent in any part of the house lately; what with the busy officer being out all day and Jakob working nights and sleeping in the afternoon they rarely saw each other. He occasionally wondered what Fischer was employed with to be out all day and return so fatigued, but as Robert was not one for telling and Jakob was not one for asking he remained none the wiser. For all of his growing fascination with the captain he was glad somewhat of his absence, as it granted the scholar full freedom of his library and study. It was in his study now that Levin eruditely worked upon his new project, oblivious even to the crash of some kind of ornament being smashed not thirty feet away – distracted by the script he was reading over, his head not three inches away from the page due to increasing myopia.

"An overseer's eye fell on the cage one day and asked the attendants why this perfectly good cage should be left standing there unused with dirty straw inside; nobody knew, until one man, helped out by a notice board, remembered about the hunger artist. They poked into the straw with sticks and found him in it. 'Are you still fasting?' asked the overseer, 'when on earth do you mean to stop?' 'Forgive me, everybody', whispered the hunger artist; only the overseer, who had his ears to the bars, understood him. 'Of course', said the overseer, and tapped his forehead with a finger to let the attendants know what state the man was in, 'we forgive you'. 'I always wanted you to admire my fasting', said the hunger artist. 'We do admire it', said the overseer, affably. 'But you shouldn't admire it', said the hunger artist. 'Well then we don't admire it', said the overseer, 'but why shouldn't we admire it' 'Because I have to fast, I can't help it', said the hunger artist. 'What a fellow you are,' said the overseer, 'and why can't you help it?' 'Because', said the hunger artist, lifting his head a little and speaking, with his lips pursed, as if for a kiss, right into the overseer's ear, so that no syllable might be lost, 'because I couldn't find the food I liked. If I had found it, believe me, I should have made no fuss and stuffed myself like you or anyone else.'"

Distress, dread and eventually relief raced through Wolfgang Nerlinger as he clumsily knocked over a crystal figurine when climbing over the table which sat next to the window. Wolfgang had tried to form a plan of attack beforehand, in that he proposed to himself that he should steal as much as possible and take particular note to search the captain's study – but our new housebreaker soon took to prowling around the room in confusion and procrastination, not knowing where to start and which valuables to take. Ornaments, paintings and silverware hung all around the would-be thief, glistening like ripened fruit upon a bough waiting to be picked. Crime does pay, Wolfgang indulgently sniggered to himself. More seriously though he justified his actions by positing that because he could transgress, he should transgress. *If you are superior then be superior.* The only law that Wolfgang recognised was evolutionary law, the survival of the fittest – and did not the old Nazi's moral transgression, transcendence, prove how fit and healthy he was? He could not help the way he was made. The only problem was that Wolfgang did not know the value of anything; he placed a gold carriage clock and a pair of silver candlesticks in his bag but then ruminated somewhat. He began to examine a couple of paintings which were prominent upon the walls, copies of Wright's 'Experiment with the Air Pump' and Holbein's 'The Ambassadors' but, again, he was ignorant of their worth; if only everything could have a price tag on it, he mused. The old buzzard of a crook was also tempted to take a reel of film which was left on the table, believing that it might have been one of those American movies with the women in translucent lingerie that the Fuhrer was rumoured to be fond of watching. After checking the draws of the cabinets Wolfgang went back and carefully placed the film in his bag.

His grip tightened vice-like around the top of his bag and with his other hand Wolfgang retrieved the pistol from his coat pocket as the burglar spied a light shining beneath the door at the end of the passage. Wolfgang was glued to the spot, not knowing whether to run and even forgetting to breathe; he stood motionless thus for a ridiculous amount of time, but then the decision was made for him.

Feeling suitably dead to the world Jakob was ready for bed – should the heavens fall he felt he could presently sleep through the drama. Looking as haggard as a drunk the wizened translator collected up his papers and rearranged the captain's desk back to the way he had found it. I do not know how much we can put it down to tiredness but, as Jakob opened the door to find a nervy Wolfgang before him, one could not have failed to be taken aback by the sheer indifference on his face. Jakob batted an eyelid, but that was all. Possessing neither a will to fight or flee, Jakob just wearily stared at Wolfgang as if he were staring into nothingness, or as if he had been expecting the felon.

"Are you alone?" the intruder desperately demanded whilst peering behind the Jew to check to see if anyone else was in the room. You could argue that Wolfgang was more taken aback by the appearance of Jakob. Not only had he expected to find the Jew still inhabiting the basement, but he hadn't expected the prisoner to look so different, human. No longer did he resemble some bug-eyed, contemplative goblin. His build and facial features had filled out and most of his hair had grown back, although it comically looked like pubic hair to some degree.

"Are you alone?" Wolfgang repeated, this time more threateningly, raising the glinting Mauser up to his eye level as he did so.

Jakob remained dully, contemptuously composed and kept his silence. Rankled, almost drooling with malice, Wolfgang marched up to the impassive Jew and slammed his boot into the Jew's hip, felling him. Drawing upon some singular strain of courage and stoicism Levin raised himself to his feet without any drama and continued to unflinchingly stare at the malodorous Nazi. Wolfgang grinned back at the insolent kike, revealing a set of canine teeth and cranberry-coloured gums.

"Shouldn't you be locked up?"

"I could ask the same question of you."

Wolfgang affected a smile, he was amused somewhat by the Jew's daring and he also didn't want to reveal how he was unsettling him – but the Nazi's nasty temper soon got the better of him and his reply was to cuff Jakob around the head with the butt of his gun, drawing blood. Still Jakob remained unfazed, oblivious even to the sensation of a tear of blood running down his cheek. At last he considered himself the author of his destiny; he would goad this dumb goy into shooting him as if he were his to command. *Death is the only true life-changing experience.* Not two days ago he had dwelled upon Socrates again, *'The hour of our departure has arrived and we go our ways – I to die and you to live. Which is better, God only knows.'*

"You should be caged up with all the other vermin."

"But then who'll be left to lock the door?"

"Don't think that I won't kill you, you ignorant kike! There is –"

"Nothing you have considered!" Levin cut in with a lifetime's worth of pent up disdain lacing his tone.

Wolfgang Nerlinger was a willing executioner. Order must, would, be restored. He was a filthy, lowly, uppity Jew, an ignoble Christ-murdering coward incapable of social, Aryan virtues. The victim should be victimised. That they could be eradicated so easily, without resistance, proved that they were fit for extinction. Even the word itself, 'Jew', brought his blood to the boil, synonymous as it was with greed, sickness and irreligion. He gripped the black, sweating handle of the Mauser tightly and narrowed his gaze.

Jakob Levin closed his eyes in anticipation, as if he were in prayer. He finally seemed at peace. Jakob even considered that should he descend into hell he would still be happy, for Sara would have made it to a heaven.

If neighbours heard the gunshot, they chose to be oblivious. Such was the age.

CHAPTER TWENTY-EIGHT

Levin violently opened his eyes to find the contorted and shocked Nazi falling towards him, slumping onto his knees and then onto the carpet. A stunned Jakob glanced up to find the captain standing before him, a similar plume of smoke pouring from his gun barrel spiralled up from the gory cavity in his assailant's back.

I cannot say how long Robert had been standing there for. He had intended to try and disarm the intruder without resulting to this, but Jakob's provocation of the old Nazi had forced his hand to act decisively. The Jew looked at the officer. Gratitude was the last thing that his features conveyed. Levin glared down at the corpse, filled with a mixture of contempt and also a dark sense of envy – for that could have now been him sleeping on the floor. Robert too found himself briefly transfixed by the slain figure, blood guzzling out of the cherry-pulp wound. He gently shook his head, as if to say "what a waste" and "what a pity"; his features burnt with a crisp sense of sorrow. Robert was angry at his own ill judgement concerning the old thug. Resentment and guilt pounded on his chest, not knowing if this resentment and guilt wanted to either enter, or leave, his heart. Frustration was unleashed. As well as ripping pieces off himself Robert was also now tempted to take it out on Jakob – for had the Jew not somehow created this chain of events? Yet sadness and grief kept him grave. He also needed to think.

"Thank you."

In its matter-of-factness Jakob's terse gratitude was almost sarcastic. Fischer gazed and ruminated upon the Jew as if he were a stranger, a freak. Robert recalled how Jakob had goaded the old Nazi – and the expression upon his face just before he was about to be shot betrayed a will to die. Should he try and save a condemned man? Robert had in the past seen them both as condemned men, shackled inexplicably to each other, but somehow the manacles had been broken. Both were indifferent to death, yes – yet Robert couldn't now assert that he was indifferent to life. Life is sacred, Robert recently judged, a belief borne more from how things should be rather than how things actually were.

"What shall we do?"

"I'll take care of it."

"Do you need me for anything?"

"No, go upstairs and get some rest."

"What will happen now?"

"He has returned to dust. We will sweep him under the carpet."

"I'm sorry," Jakob replied mechanically.

*

Despite the inhospitable hour Robert left a message for General Haber to get in contact with him urgently. Not thinking twice that he was swallowing his pride, Robert called in his favours and the general was able to dispose of the nameless corpse without the police getting involved. Suffice to say nothing became of Wolfgang Nerlinger after his demise.

CHAPTER TWENTY-NINE

Time passes.

Robert had been expecting it, but nevertheless shock and grief thumped upon his heart and a lump rose up in his throat. No day without tears.

"All Jews in custody and employment are to be terminated."

So ordered the dispatch that was delivered to an unnerving number of military and civilian personnel at the close of the war. It would have been easy and natural for the officer to fall into a gloom – so too a year ago Robert might have reacted with placid insouciance – but work had to be done. Inertly dwelling upon his responsibility would do no one any good.

*

Jakob Levin gazed out of the window and could not help but be impressed by the powers of German automotive engineering. Everything but the kitchen sink had been loaded onto the caravan of trucks and cars which were migrating west. Horns were hoarse, curses were traded, traffic congealing like a scab along the avenue. Where were their proud social virtues of loyalty and duty now? The master race had its tale between its legs – out-witted and out-fought by the 'Bolshevik sub-human scum'. Not without a triumphal air he looked down upon the crestfallen procession. And what was Hitler doing now? Jakob called him the 'Bunyip' – in aboriginal folk-lore it was a man-eating bellowing monster that abducted his victims and dragged them down to his cave at the bottom of a swamp. So too the word is used to mean impostor.

"Rats leaving a sinking ship," Jakob asserted out loud to himself.

The war was all but over, the Russians were coming. He hadn't permitted it before, but Jakob pondered on what he would do after the fighting. He smiled wistfully, because he knew the answer. He would do that which he had done before and during the war, he would sit in a dimly lit room and translate whatever happened to be in front of him. Should another chapter of war open up – and Jakob had every faith in pessimism that it would – he would no doubt just continue to do the same. Teaching even held no appeal for Levin now. He mumbled underneath his breath, resignation mixed with revelation, quoting Goethe.

> *'I take no pleasure in anything now;*
> *For I know I know nothing, I wonder how*
> *I can still keep up this pretence of teaching*
> *Or bettering mankind with my empty preaching.*
> *Can I even boast of any worldly success?*
> *What fame or riches do I possess?*

No dog would put up with such an existence!"

Captain Fischer cleaned and loaded his pistol, taking a particular interest in the last bullet which he placed directly into the recently oiled chamber. He checked the time, it was nine o'clock. Although it was far from sultry or the hottest day of the year, it seemed the hottest. The heavy uniform only exacerbated his clamminess but still the taut officer kept all the buttons done up, parade style. After signing to report that he had received and carried out the order the captain gravely rose and ventured up to the master bedroom from his muggy office. Duty called.

*

Jakob was far from superstitious but he had woken to a presentiment that the day would somehow be important – that something would somehow happen. Of course superstition but played half a part in Levin's presentiment; he was not innocent of the idea that the state might issue the order to have him executed, nor was Jakob oblivious to the proximity of the Russian army. He caught the sound of someone in the corridor.

Robert realised just how much he was sweating when his hand slipped off the brass handle in his attempt to open the door. The officer, in a formal nod, acknowledged Jakob. Jakob returned the subdued greeting with a thin, impersonal smile. Since the evening of the shooting the pair had barely spoken to each other. Even at the best of times the two articulate men had little to say. So too their respective routines – that of Robert being absent for most of the day and Levin translating through the night – meant that they continued to spend little time in each other's company. It was an arrangement not particularly disquieting for either of them.

"Are you ready?"

Jakob put his pen down and carefully marked his place in his book.

"Is it time?"

"Yes."

Robert and Jakob had briefly spoken about the eventualities some time ago (Robert had talked, Jakob had listened). The prisoner passively followed the captain downstairs and into that basement cum cell that he had once inhabited. It was the first time that Levin had been back down here and, for a brief moment, his aspect betrayed flecks of distress. The room called back harsh memories, but Jakob reeled in his self; this gloomy basement would now serve as his salvation, not purgatory.

Abraham Solomon had made Robert's task easier in that he had already commenced what seemed to be a hideaway underneath the house. While investigating the possibility of constructing a trap door and sanctuary for Jakob, the officer discovered a false plaster surface covering up a hole about two feet deep spooned into the floor. Hiring an ex-soldier and carpenter, Robert had completed the project and although not fool-proof from detection, the captain was suitably confident of Jakob's safety should he not return from where he was going. It was because of Robert's apprehension that he might not return that he had decided to hide Jakob now.

Robert used a specially filed crow bar to find the edge of the door and lifted up the concrete slab which served as an entrance to the alcove. Jakob peered into it. The secret chamber was about two and a half metres long, two metres wide and a metre and a half high, or deep. Inside Levin could spy a mattress, his old toilet, various provisions, a lamp, some candles and a pistol.

"I hope it will be sufficient. You may have to stay hidden for anything up to two weeks."

"I shall ration my provisions. Do you wish me to go in right now?"

"I do not know when I will be coming back and I need to disguise the entrance. If I am unable to return then I suggest that you do not come out immediately at the sound of Russian voices as they might be looters. If you can wait for the British, they will know what to do and will treat you justly."

Both men, Anglophiles, smiled, appreciating the sense and unspoken sentiment.

Jakob had intended to ask about Charlotte. He sensed that something had happened between them, but affairs of the heart had never been the translator's metier. Charlotte had written informing Jakob that she would see him again – the captain too had assured him of the same. Jakob climbed down into the shelter, his chest and head still protruding out of the hole. He clutched his papers next to his stomach as if they formed some kind of comfort blanket for the ageing Jew, but otherwise his diffident and passive expression was not altogether that different from that to when he first stood, meekly squinting, in Robert's office.

"You might wish to light the lamp or one of the candles first before I replace the tile, otherwise it might prove too dark."

"Thank you."

A slight pause occurred as if neither character knew whose turn it was to speak. Jakob was indeed only prompted into action after Robert picked up the stone slab which served as the covering.

"Well, if I do not see you again, goodbye Jakob."

Perhaps it was due to the fact that Jakob realised that he might never see the captain again - but he somehow snapped out of his trance and regained that philosophical nobility of soul that he had lost in his youth — for he could not wholly blame the Reich for that sin. Tears glistened in his eyes and his face beamed with a singular spirit. He stepped back out of the hole.

"Goodbye, and thank you. God be with you, Robert. You are a good man."

Robert Fischer couldn't help but be touched by the friendship and humanity in Jakob's tone.

"Do you know that is the first time you have called me by my name?"

"I know. And I apologise."

"Next to your bed down there is a letter. You must promise me Jakob that should anything happen to me you will follow its instructions. You must now promise me, give me your word."

Instead of answering Jakob dug out a pencil, impulsively tore a piece of paper off his manuscript, wrote something down and handed it to the officer.

"You must first promise me something. Upon this piece of paper is a name and number. Hand it into the office at Dresden train station. They should hand you a key for a locker. In it you'll find a box. It would make both my wife and I happy, and honoured, if you kept the contents – my wedding ring and my wife's Bible. Please Captain, Robert. I would like them to have a good home," Jakob pleaded, anticipating an objection.

Tears, either of joy or grief, can be infectious. Mutual admiration and affection shone from both of their countenances - albeit the two contrasting men admired each other for different, unarticulated reasons.

"It will be my honour," Robert replied after a pause, stifled a little by the emotion in his voice.

"Goodbye and thank you Robert," Jakob warmly remarked, holding out his limp hand to the younger man. Grateful.

"Goodbye, Jakob."

The Captain held the trap door under one arm and with his free hand, wiping it first on his trousers as if he was meeting royalty, Robert exchanged a firm and warm handshake with the rabbinical Jew. Love and an affinity passed between the two men; they somehow knew that they would never see each other again, but both also knew that they would be no unhappier or lonelier for spending the rest of their lives apart. The two men would always feel somewhat distant, different - it was one of the traits they had in common.

Jakob descended into the shelter and Robert carefully placed the tile over him. The niggarding doubts that Fischer had in that the light from the shelter might somehow shine up from the hole thankfully proved unfounded.

Although Jakob was only fleetingly entombed in darkness before he lit a stubby candle, a memory was ignited from when he was a teenager. He'd had another fight with his father, either about him reading one of his philosophy books instead of the passages he was instructed to memorise from the Talmud – or had the argument and punishment ensued from when, even though physically beaten by his father, he still stood there Roman-like and claimed he was more German than Jewish? Dragging him down the stairs, his pale face damp with tears, his father thought it might teach Jakob a lesson to be locked in the cupboard under the banisters without food or light for the rest of the day. Initially the young stoic bore his lamentations with fortitude and refused to give his orthodox father the satisfaction of apologising or seeing that he could alter his convictions. But his time spent isolated in the cobwebbed cupboard – where no aspect could become accustomed to the dark and the fifteen year old couldn't even see his hand in front of his face – wore on like the hours of eternity. His eyes were rarely dry from tears of self-pity, or indignation. Then, as now, a verse from the Bible solemnly recalled itself to Jakob:

"I wait for your deliverance Lord."

And then, as now, the wondering Jew didn't quite know if he wanted the Lord to come and save him – or to just deliver him from this illogical, bleeding world. Maybe one now meant the other for the remorseful academic.

CHAPTER THIRTY

The artillery fire rumbled in the distance, like thunder. Occasional tongues of fire tasted the air above the rooftops of distant buildings. Smoke choked out sunlight, rising like the old industrial plumes and clouds which used to bellow out from the now bombed out Krupp factories on the outskirts of town. Abrasive machine gun fire reverberated in the air like the sound of clattering rattles at a football match.

Robert purposefully strode up the slight gradient of Grimm Avenue, the sun upon his back. He was on his way to the town square and cathedral, or rather the makeshift hospital he had funded and worked in these past weeks. The town's authorities had discussed the project of turning the cathedral into an annexe of the hospital but nothing had actually been done about it. In stepped the wealthy officer. The captain provided the institution with the necessary capital and the hospital furnished Robert with the necessary supplies, advice and staff. Robert looked after the finances and administration while Michael Scholl, the auxiliary hospital's only fully qualified doctor, organised and attended to the medical care. At present the giant ward housed around seventy patients, mainly casualties from the Front. The staff at the hospital also consisted of six nurses who worked their three shifts in pairs and, upon this day, the cathedral was also the posting to two young privates who had been ordered to assist Captain Fischer in guarding the medical facility. Robert was worried that the Russian army would be as respectful to Germany as the Wehrmacht and SS had been to the rest of Eastern Europe. He was worried for the lives and belongings of the patients – and the nurses; it would be because and not in spite of the cathedral being a sacred place that it could become a focal point for Russian retribution.

Robert figured that he might have to hold off the marauding Russians for as much as half a day until such a time that the Red Army could impose a certain order upon itself; so too it depended on the town's official declaration of surrender. Robert again prayed that the British might somehow arrive. He advised himself that perhaps the best course of action to take would be to surrender; if he could locate a Russian officer then he might be able to bribe him and purchase fair treatment for the patients. Robert turned his thoughts again to the two virtuous nurses and the unthinkable; he was hopeful but also realistic; it was not because they were Russians that he was a feared for the women, it was because they were men. Unsurprisingly Robert also spared a thought for Charlotte, still achingly beautiful and moral in his mind. How often had he dreamed that Charlotte might somehow find out about his work and visit him, or better still he sketched scenarios of them meeting accidentally after the war. Things would be different. The wounds were still tender, scars had yet to heal – but maybe one day in the future they might... Robert yearned to confess to her how she had partly been his inspiration for the hospital. Could she one day understand and forgive him? Could he one day understand and forgive himself? He shook his head, dismissing the notion. Even if they could just be friends. Perhaps Robert loved her all the more now that he had lost her, but because he loved Charlotte he would live without her. There was goodness, but sadness, in his heart.

I miss her.

Part of Robert's self-imposed brief when taking over the cathedral had been to restore and maintain the statue of Christ. Secretly, it was the task the officer was proudest of. Every day, before entering the cathedral, Robert peered up at the figure. The mystery was no longer a mystery. Faith illuminates.

Christ was not the only one who had his eyes on Robert now though as he approached the cathedral. So too Hermann Vole, the town official assigned to the administration of the hospital, could not take his bespectacled eyes off the captain. Hermann Vole was only four years older than Robert Fischer but his proclivity to worry about any and everything had aged him considerably. His lank hair had thinned; his back was hunched like that of an old man. One could often find him squinting in divination over the most trivial of matters – or he would screw up his eyes because the light was either too bright or too dim. A pinched and resentful expression sometimes haunted his countenance, both in public and in private, derived from the bureaucrat pondering on what might have been if the war, which he had initially supported, had not broken out. Herr Vole scratched his inner thigh and then neck, drawing a blotch of blood from taking a head of a pimple. His nervous rash had flared up again, but this time for good reason.

It could've been argued that Hermann Vole owned two modes of being. When he was addressing what he and society considered his superior in station Hermann would defer to them religiously – he could swallow his pride as easy as chum. The angst of Hermann Vole's social castration was sublimated however through his persona of the officious tyrant who would round on any inferior who did not adhere to his standards concerning official policies and laws from on high. The socialist was merely a vessel for the all-powerful state.

Relief that the captain had finally arrived – and understandable distress – chequered Vole's ferret-like features. All that morning the administrator had been clucking around the cathedral like a headless chicken. He frequently annoyed the nurses by questioning what they were doing and then replying, "Yes, good job" or "Yes, you carry on with that". A fretful Hermann also unfailingly succeeded in disturbing the anxious patients by reassuring them that they would be safe when the Russians came. "This is a house of God and medical instillation, I doubt not that they will treat us honourably, don't you think?" Five minutes later the unofficial morale officer began to distribute Bibles to the patients. Thankfully for the patients Hermann's rounds were cut short by the arrival of the two young privates that General Haber had promised Robert. Such was the pristine state of their uniforms that their mothers could not have but two hours ago finished ironing them – Michael Scholl thought to himself. Teenaged, florid faced and gangly, they neither inspired confidence in themselves or the fatalistic patients. Herr Vole however immediately pestered these two newest of recruits as to the situation on the outskirts of town. The truth, which the freshly conscripted boy-soldiers were innocent of, would have unsettled the official even more than his imagination's intelligence regarding the doom-laden defensive. After delivering various pearls of wisdom to a young casualty who had recently had his left foot shot off, such as "Life goes on" and "Believe it or not but I know how you feel to some extent", Hermann Vole had spent the last half hour fervently looking out for Captain Fischer, as if he were a ship-wrecked sailor looking for a mast on the horizon. Upon finally observing the captain across the town square Hermann sighed, in a parody almost of a sigh, with relief.

"Good morning Hermann, I apologise for my being late."

"What are we going to do, Captain?" the former municipal officer once in charge of public lavatories replied. Upon hearing the captain's equitable composure he felt that he needed to sound worried for the both of them.

"Tell the staff and patients that I will make an announcement presently."

Herr Vole was a little aggrieved not to be party to the captain's plan before the rest of the hospital, but he nevertheless dutifully marched in front of the captain and herald-like informed one and all that the captain was present, which they could all plainly see for themselves. He formally pronounced that Captain Fischer was going to make an announcement. Although one could've heard a pin drop, Hermann also asked for quiet.

The half-church half-hospital seemed exactly that. The altar and lectern still stood in place and about a third of the space was still taken up by pews but in between there sublimely lived an auxiliary hospital ward. As Robert calmly walked down the aisle so to speak he might have noticed how the building was even infused with the various distinctive aromas of a church and hospital. Perfumed candles, disinfectant, blood, stone, gangrene and such like permeated the air.

The patients that could prop themselves up on their beds did so. Some of them thought the captain aloof, some of them cynically explained his generosity as being an easy form of compensation for his cowardice, but most of them had increasingly grown to like the man. He was friendly without being patronising and never once gave the impression that he should somehow be congratulated for his work and charity; although the captain often kept himself to himself he never once took his melancholic moods out on people and acted as if the world revolved around him, unlike a list of other officers that the men had suffered under.

Robert glanced about him to gauge the atmosphere of the group and to check to see if he had everyone's attention. He noticed his two callow recruits. The thought that this terrible conflict was nearly over for the youths comforted him in his sorrow, although it was far from consolation enough. But the officer did not wish to sow diffidence into the teenagers and he smiled at them in a reassuring and appreciative manner.

"I apologise for my being late people, but I shit my pants this morning upon receiving the news that the Russians were coming."

The nervous and stolid-faced patients couldn't help but laugh. The nurses smiled and blushed when the handsome officer looked at them to witness the success of his ice-breaker, which almost magically immersed the hospital in a more spirited and relaxed mood.

"The plan is that we will transfer ourselves down into the cathedral's crypt. There should be sufficient room. These two young gentlemen and I will then attempt to barricade you in. Hopefully, if the fighting does not endure for too long a time, a certain order will be restored to the town. You would not believe me if I said that everything was going to be fine, nor would I want you to, but I do believe we have reason to be confident."

More than the captain's speech, fears were forgotten due to the practical tasks at hand which people busied their selves with. More than anyone else it was the patients who got the work done. Genuine usefulness, for a worthy cause, should not be underestimated as a source of motivation. During transporting the immobile casualties and equipment down into the crypt, Robert took time out to give a few words of encouragement to the two privates who were under his command. Although unrelated the pair looked as identical as brothers or cousins – beardless, mouths agape and gulping at the slightest unsightly image, their eyes sucking in the gory scenes. Their ears pricked to attention however as their captain informally addressed them.

"Save your energy boys, there's no need to salute me...Today we must be as bold as Beauchamp. In 1346 Thomas Beauchamp, the Earl of Warwick, accompanied by one squire and six archers, defeated a hundred armed men in Hogges, Normandy. Now I know they had the advantage of their enemy being French, but we must be equally bold against our enemy today. I have every faith in your abilities and courage, even if you might doubt what you're made of. Stay focused and remember your training. I'll cut your rations and dock your pay in an instant if either of you get yourselves killed today, understand?" the officer said with a grin, easing the tension in the faces of the boy-soldiers too.

The confidence of the two youths, who stuck together like glue, was buoyed by their captain's faith in them. Moreover their chins were up and chests out due to the way two modestly pretty nurses began to gaze upon them. If nothing else these squires would fight for the honour of these maidens.

Robert also took Michael Scholl aside. The two men had garnered a mutual respect for each other over the past couple of months.

"Michael, may I have a word?"

"Certainly, Captain."

"As a precaution, I thought that we might arm those patients who are willing and able. I would also ask you to take special care —"

"I know, all the men will make sure the nurses are looked after."

"Thank you."

Michael Scholl here motioned to take his leave of the captain but he then turned back, suddenly remembering something he wished to communicate.

"People are wrong about you Captain, I'd just like you to know that."

Robert was going to reply that "they were right, and that is why they are now wrong", but he considered that the fruits of his conversion were more important than the history of it. Before the officer had a chance to thank the Doctor however, who had done a job above and beyond the call of duty over the past months, the pair were interrupted. The Doctor rushed to help a one-eyed man struggling to carry the hospital's precious supply of morphine and the officer was similarly distracted as he helped a patient on crutches who had dropped his Bible.

Hermann Vole made the token gesture of volunteering to remain by the captain's side and fight off the Russians. He protested and was all the more willing to do his duty when the officer made it clear that he would by no means accept his offer, explaining that he needed the official to do the more essential job of looking after the patients.

"Let the fellow fight, he could bombard the Russians with paperwork."

"Yeah, death by a thousand paper cuts!" a couple of the patients joked, to a chorus of approval and laughter.

"Ignore them, Captain," Hermann replied with a self-important air – and audibly enough so that his uncouth and disfigured critics could hear.

"Listen men, do not underestimate our Hermann's usefulness," the captain announced, much to the satisfaction of the pompous official, "he could well be our secret weapon. If the Russians look like breaking through our defences, intent on harm, I want you to do to them what you have tried to do to our men, Hermann. Bore them to death."

Hermann's face was a picture. His lips were sourly pursed as if they had just been sewn together with a needle and thread. His fall was all the more arresting from the captain – and his own ego – having built him up. The room exploded with hale and hearty laughter. Robert himself even smiled broadly but was quick to offer an apology to the butt of his joke.

"I'm sorry Hermann, but take heart that you have provided the men with some comic relief."

Herr Vole forced a smile for his superior, but brooded and subsequently took his mood out on everyone else.

Sunlight hammered upon him. Robert undid the buttons on his jacket. Blotches of sweat soaked his shirt and skin. The temperature was magnified by the decorative stained glass window, of Christ weeping on the cross, which hung above the officer. Such was the incandescent light that it illuminated the motes of dust proliferating the air, enamelling them into silver – and such was the oppression of the stinging heat that it was almost a tangible weight upon the soldier's back.

Late afternoon. Dusk was stirring, yawning and about to awake. The bass of the throbbing Russian artillery had recently become punctuated with the staccato refrain of machine gun fire. Robert asked his two privates to keep watch at the front of the cathedral in case casualties turned up, as well as keeping watch for the Russians. The captain was positioned behind the upturned altar; the sizeable cypress table, with a sheet of gold plated steel covering its surface like a blanket, served as a perfect defensive shield. The anxious officer gulped down some more brackish water from his canteen and continued to check and sort his grand army's ammo and weaponry. As if on cue, as soon as Robert finished this task he was disturbed by the conscientious and fretful voice of one of his privates.

"Captain, Captain."

Robert picked up his MP40 and hurried towards the door, his pulse quickening with each step. Twenty yards or so from the entrance the officer and his two privates had erected a barricade consisting of a knotted line of the cathedral's pews and any other useful, useless debris that they could lay their hands on to shore up their defences. Robert also lined some of the barricade with barbed wire and fishing line – in order to fool the enemy that the defences were booby-trapped. Robert easily negotiated his own barrier however by slipping through a disguised and designated opening on the left side of their improvised fortification.

"It's one of our men, Captain."

Coriolanus was not covered in so much blood, yet the malnourished Wehrmacht sergeant wore neither pride nor glory in his face. But how heroic had been the feat to reach the hospital, with half of his rhubarb intestines cradled in his hands? His face was a warped mixture of agony and relief, as if the cathedral signified salvation. The two privates, overcoming their fear, rushed out into the town square to act as crutches for the casualty. Groaning vehicles and stubble-faced soldiers scrambled about in the background. Russian smoke and fire had infiltrated the German hive, throwing its inhabitants into a frenzy, or daze. Upon reaching the officer, before slipping into unconsciousness, the wounded sergeant summoned up all his reserves of strength to report to the captain.

"Behind me," the casualty croaked, as if blood were bubbling up from the roots of his lungs. It was as if the message he delivered was as important as him reaching the hospital. He had earned his rest.

"You two wait here for any other casualties. I'm just going to retrieve the medical kit I put aside for the wounded."

The captain knew that the gesture of trying to revive the shot messenger would be tantamount to a rain dance in a time of drought, but Robert would nevertheless attempt to dress the Sergeant's injuries and make him as comfortable as possible. Charlotte had been right, "just because it is a losing battle that does not mean that you should not fight it". He raced back towards the altar of the cathedral, panting as the devoted husband and father drew his last rasping breath.

The adolescent recruits were nameless but they should not be forgotten. Not only did fate seem to stab them in the back but, as if in some final flourish to its work, fate twisted the knife into the two conscripts. The message of "Behind me" referred to the imminent arrival of oncoming Russians, not wounded Germans.

Robert had taught them the phrase "We surrender" in Russian – but even if one of the youths had been able to shoot it out the volley of fire would have still hammered into his chest, shredding it like carrots upon a grater. I wish I could say that the Russians were not themselves, that war had addled their hearts and it was all blood-lust, but they were in sufficient possession of their minds and wills. One can defend them by saying is it not just that they should do unto the Germans what the Germans did unto them? One can but one shouldn't. Justice is mercy.

About ten of them had broken off from their unit. Savagery gleamed in their bearded, sallow faces. "Not even National Socialism, or Bertrand Russell, could edify them" – Jorge Albetz had once satirically remarked to Robert.

Robert did not have time to mourn the tragic deaths of the two boys. The Russians swarmed through the door like children rushing downstairs at Christmas; the rogue unit imagined that somewhere in the building there must have lived a room full of valuables and provisions. When the berserkers were half way between the entrance of the cathedral and the makeshift barricade Robert opened fire, deliberately shooting over the heads of the enemy.

The soldiers scattered like ants, with Robert providing the boiling water. The robber band of Russians ducked their heads and took cover, half of them retreating back to the door, the other half taking cover behind the line of pews. In imperfect Russian Robert began to speak to his congregation.

"This building is now officially a hospital. Where is your

commanding officer?"

"I am an officer, now come out and surrender."

"Yes, I am an officer too. You will be safe."

"You fool" and "just let me do the talking" could also be heard to emanate from the unsupervised soldiers.

"Even if there is not an officer among you, under the terms of the –"

Realising that somehow their duplicity had failed, that there was perhaps only a single guard left behind the table – and also from general frustration and adrenaline – the front ranks positioned their rifles through gaps in the pews and opened fire.

The berating din of the volley was made worse by the acoustics of the cathedral. Robert had fully expected this outcome, but only the experience itself could have prepared him for the near nerve-shattering tumult. Even Hector himself would have, like our Captain, crouched himself into a ball, put his hands over his head, and rode out the deafening maelstrom of fire. Lightning owned more chance of hitting the mark however, shielded as Robert was behind the upturned table. It was as if the Devil himself was rapping upon the other side of the table top though, spitting fire and clapping with joy.

"Surrender and we will let you live my friend, or we will cut you to ribbons. If you do not surrender now, I will not be responsible for my actions. You have one minute, friend."

Robert peered through one of the various spy holes that he had drilled into the table and assessed the grim situation. During their recent attack the men who had retreated to the door re-joined their comrades. Through the mesh of his barricade Robert counted eleven men. It would be more than likely that reinforcements for this robber band would arrive before any officer, and what guarantee of safety would there be if such an officer arrived? Surrender was not an option and bribery would but defer for five minutes the fatal outcome that surrender entailed. Robert would have to fight, attack being the best form of defence. Even though out-numbered and out-gunned he was confident of his short-term survival from his holding of the superior position. He instructed himself, as if he were master and pupil, to keep his senses sharp and remember his training. He took a couple of deep, cooling breaths, mopped his saturated brow with his sleeve, and made his reply to the ultimatum.

"What is your decision my friend?"

"I will now give you a minute to retreat and leave this hospital, before you become one of its wounded."

A couple of the Russians couldn't help but repeat the German's bravado to each other and laugh. But before they had a chance to enter into their second bar of laughter Robert opened fire, spraying rounds down upon them from over the table. A machine gun will often fire a man rather than a man will fire it, but Robert was strong and composed enough to tame the report of the wriggling MP40 and deliberately aim downwards. Chips flew up from the pews like chaff from a thresher and molten hot bullets cut into the legs of a few of the Russians, scything them down. Trying to blot the piercing screams out of his mind Robert ceased firing and took cover again. Those that could returned fire. So too one of the infantrymen – enraged by the shooting of his close comrade and the blood lust of storming the town – managed to scramble through a gap in the barricade. If he hadn't been so vocal and enraged perhaps the daring Russian might have achieved his aim but his cliché war cry alerted the German to his charge. The Russian's revenge mission became a suicidal one. He fired a clumsy shot which was directed well above Robert's head. From the pitch and crescendo of the wail Robert didn't need to gaze through one of his spy holes. He swiftly got up, barely registering the round which hissed over his head, briefly closed his eyes as if already in a prayer for forgiveness – and squeezed the trigger. Robert ducked back behind the cover of the table as swiftly as he had risen from above it. No sooner did he do so than the rest of the man's unit returned fire, pouring out the violence in their hearts and emptying their rifles. Robert tried to catch his breath and smashed the butt of his gun upon the stone floor in anger and grief. He was damned if he did and damned if he didn't kill the Russian youth. His face was waxen and his eyes bulged as if he had shed a tear for every day he had been on this Godforsaken planet.

The solitary German and the Russians continued to trade fire on and off for about another hour, with the German officer parrying rather than thrusting. At one point he became worried when he heard the order that one of the men should try to obtain a hand grenade but, with it failing to materialize, Robert had reason to believe he could sustain the stalemate.

"In the name of God, what is going on here?!"

The authoritative voice unmistakably belonged to an officer, yet pity as much as indignation was imbued in its tone. Robert eagerly looked through one of his peepholes and discovered that a commanding officer had indeed arrived, attended by a dozen of his men. Robert also witnessed to his relief the Russians behind the line of pews lower their weapons; he briefly closed his eyes again, but this time in a prayer of thanks rather than forgiveness.

"My name is Captain Robert Fischer. This building is officially a hospital. Do I have your word that, should I surrender, you will treat the patients and staff justly?"

"You have my word, Captain." His accent was as much European as Russian, Robert briefly fancied.

In a gesture of good faith Robert slid one of his guns away from him. He first raised his hands, perched upon aching arms, and then the rest of the officer appeared from behind the scarred and blistered altar table which had served him so solidly. By now the Russian commander had climbed through a gap in Robert's defences.

"I am Captain Ivan Radomsky. You speak good Russian."

"Reading Dostoyevsky in his native language was a good incentive."

"The reason why I taught myself German was to read Shakespeare in his native language," the Russian joked in unassumingly perfect German.

Captain Radomsky's face, in its friendliness and handsome appeal, egressed warmth and ability. Even though the harpy of philosophy and his university education had tried, Ivan Antov

Radomsky, as if in possession of some simple faith which was immune to the sophistications of the intellect, could even smile in the face of that Hydra Irony. He had bested the moral cancer that had eaten away, like frostbite, the humanity of so many of his comrades during the course of the war. The famed Stalingrad sniper, who could have been no older than twenty-five, was fair-haired and possessed a natural air of sincerity and virtue. The breadth of his sense of humour was only matched by his intelligence – and his bright eyes bespoke of that secret, uncorrupted wisdom whose first precept is to admit of one's ignorance and humility. Radomsky, with his strong features and agility, was like some force of all that was good in nature – which is not to say that he was a stranger to the nature of Nietzsche and Darwin. But even the war could not defeat the good humour and individual humanity of the Russian Captain, both because and in spite of the suffering and sins he had seen and experienced. Radomsky grinned and shook the opposing officer's hand as if he had known him all his life. Robert couldn't help but be impressed by the honourable Russian officer. He had appeared as miraculously as a rainbow – and seemed as colourful, too. He issued orders with familiarity but also authority and his men, even the embittered, know- it- all- war dogs, seemed to obey him willingly.

Granted, Robert perhaps here bestowed upon the captain such Christian and valiant qualities that he could not have possibly divined at first sight – but Robert instantly trusted and respected the superior officer. He recognised in the Russian Captain that young man who he could have been, who he still wanted to be. Relief coursed through his veins. His hospital would be safe in his hands.

Perhaps it was because of all the excitement and exhaustion but the delirious thought dawned upon Robert that Ivan Radomsky deserved to marry Charlotte. Buffeted between conceit and the sublime the revelation seemed to last both for a moment and an eternity. A heaven on earth would be created by the union. He gave the match his blessing, smiling upon the idea fondly and with paternal pride. They could, would, make a fitting couple.

Radomsky noticed how clammy the German's hand was as he shook it, and how feverish his countenance seemed. Ivan had witnessed shell shock and trauma manifest itself in a variety of ways but yet the Russian Captain was not prone to morbidity, nor did he wish to worry over nothing. There was warmth as well as wildness in the German's aspect; he could appreciate the euphoric relief that he must have been feeling. The Russian schoolteacher only became a little disconcerted at the officer's state of mind when the German asked him the following singular question.

"Are you married, Captain?"

We should consider the lowly Russian infantryman to be duteous or loyal. His youthful comrade had attacked the Nazi out of a sense of revenge for when he himself had been shot in the leg. The boy had looked up to the veteran soldier ever since he had first taken him under his wing in Rostov. The old soldier had felt touched and indebted to the boy, who had even parted with part of his nugget ration of bread when the veteran was ill.

That he should be slain so near to the end of the war compounded the tragedy. Fired by an age-old equation of justice of an eye for an eye the veteran vowed to honour his comrade's memory and kill his killer. To hell with the consequences and to hell with this soft German-loving officer, who had thwarted his unit's plans to loot the Cathedral.

Even the heart of the avenging marksman stopped for a second. The knell seemed to echo in the church's air for an age. The bullet thudded into Robert's chest like a fist; blood splattered over the Russian Captain like mud.

The force of the shot shoved the German backwards – but still he somehow managed to stay on his feet. Shock more than anything else shaped his features. His shirt became drenched in blood in seconds. The rest of the world was sucked into the background as Robert's fiery red hand loomed large in front of his glazed eyes. Robert continued to stagger backwards until he leant upon the altar. The back of his head propped itself and was caught on the table's edge, supporting his weight. Strangely, feverishly, Robert, as well as remaining on his feet, continued his train of thought concerning Charlotte and the gallant Russian. His dream became as heated as his wound; with a diabolical fervour the dying romantic became possessed by the idea that they must marry, else the town, Europe, would rot like an apple. His breathing became shallow. The tracks soon failed to run parallel below his train of thought however. His life flashed before him. Pleasure, grief and guilt. The world grew ever dimmer and blurred – and delirium manifested itself as the officer began to ramble like an idiot, or a dying man.

"Yes, never… Sorry, sorry. I am dead Horatio… She's lonely.

Dark." He mumbled as his head nodded and swayed as if set upon a pivot.

Robert winced in agony. As diseased as his consciousness was, one could trace in his features a defiance to stay awake. The sweat and blood which not a minute ago felt warm and sticky now chilled his frame. His bleached face twitched, his lips and limbs trembled. When the hopes and paradisal vistas mutated into macabre nightmares Robert might have wished himself dead. Should Ivan Radomsky and Charlotte not marry, the dying man saw, with deranged clarity, the apocalyptic Dragon and voluptuous Whore of Babylon standing at the altar – and a lightless world filled with their progeny of satyrs and harlots. Each breath now was masochism for the German, speech was tantamount to an act of heroism. Dusk was decomposing, losing out to night's inevitable reign. It seemed to take a lifetime for Radomsky to reach the German officer but he hastily called for a medi-kit and keenly bent over to listen to this honourable Captain, instinctively feeling that he had something important to say.

"Marry…," Robert whispered into his ear.

The older man had intended to say "Marry Charlotte Friedrich", somehow believing that all which was needed was for Ivan and Charlotte to meet. But the life ebbed out of the officer before the words. Robert Fischer's prayer went to the grave with him. What was left of the falling light poetically refracted through the elliptical stained glass window and illuminated a contorted face.

This chapter ends, as all chapters end.

ACKNOWLEDGEMENTS

The bulk of this novel was written well over a decade ago. I was so much younger then, I'm older than that now, to misquote Bob Dylan.

In terms of a source of information and inspiration I can recommend the following books, in regards to further reading. First and foremost there is Mikhail's Lermontov's *A Hero of our Time*. The writings of both Kierkegaard and Nietzsche were prominent among my bookshelves, as well as those of Robert Fischer's, when producing this novel too. There are numerous non-fiction works about the Third Reich, which will have the power to shock, anger, stimulate and depress you – but I can especially recommend Michael Burleigh's *The Third Reich: A New History*, *Defying Hitler* by Sebastien Haffner, Ian Kershaw's *The End* and Roger Moorhouse's *Berlin At War*.

Also, should you have enjoyed *A Hero of Our Time*, you may be interested in reading *Warsaw*, another novel set during the Second World War.

Please also feel free to get in touch via richard@endeavourpress. com or @rforemanauthor on twitter.

ENDEAVOUR INK

Endeavour Ink is an imprint of Endeavour Press.

If you enjoyed *A Hero of Our Time* check out
Endeavour Press's eBooks here:
www.endeavourpress.com

For weekly updates on our free and discounted eBooks sign up
to our newsletter:
www.endeavourpress.com

Follow us on Twitter:
@EndeavourPress